Sid Junior paused, and Betty knew that something else was coming. "Betty, maybe while you're up there, you can talk to Mother, convince her that a nursing home would be best for him. He always listened to you."

Yes, he did, Betty thought, but no, I will not become involved in the Edwardses' personal business . . . and I don't agree that a nursing home is the answer. . . .

"We'll discuss it when I get there," Betty said.

"Good," Junior said. "Having him around at home all the time, knowing he understands everything, even if he can't speak, is holding me back from what I want to do. A nursing home would be the ideal solution."

Junior's ideal solution, Betty realized sadly, was to see his father dead. . . .

By Joyce Christmas
Published by Fawcett Books:

Lady Margaret Priam mysteries:
A FÊTE WORSE THAN DEATH
SUDDENLY IN HER SORBET
SIMPLY TO DIE FOR
A STUNNING WAY TO DIE
FRIEND OR FAUX
IT'S HER FUNERAL
A PERFECT DAY FOR DYING
MOURNING GLORIA

Betty Trenka mysteries:
THIS BUSINESS IS MURDER
DEATH AT FACE VALUE
DOWNSIZED TO DEATH

DOWNSIZED TO DEATH

A Betty Trenka Mystery

Joyce Christmas

FAWCETT GOLD MEDAL • NEW YORK

A Fawcett Gold Medal Book
Published by Ballantine Books
Copyright © 1997 by Joyce Christmas

http://www.randomhouse.com

Library of Congress Catalog Number: 97-90575

ISBN: 0-449-14802-5

Manufactured in the United States of America

First Edition: November 1997

10 9 8 7 6 5 4 3 2

For Alyce Bohannon

Friend, fan, phenomenon,
and most of all, a reader

CHAPTER 1

BETTY TRENKA accepted with equanimity the white cardboard envelope with the bold purple and orange logo: FEDEX. The young Federal Express deliveryman pointed to the line on his clipboard where she was to sign, tapped some numbers and letters into his handheld device, and dashed back to his truck parked on the shoulder of Timberhill Road in front of her house.

It was exactly nine-thirty on an unexpectedly warm Tuesday in February. Betty approved of companies that lived up to their promises. FedEx promised nine-thirty delivery, and here was her overnight letter, from . . .

Her equanimity evaporated at the sight of the printed return address: Edwards & Son. 31 Maple Street. Grafton, Connecticut.

In the six months since she had reluctantly retired from Edwards & Son (been told to retire by Sid Edwards Junior, if the truth be known), Betty had heard not a word from anyone at the company where she had labored for some thirty-seven years. Well, they'd sent her a W-2 form last month for the previous year's earnings, but no message. She'd written Sid Senior a note out in Arizona in the midst of his equally unwelcome retirement after

1

she had gotten settled, but there had been no reply. She'd figured sadly that keeping in touch was not something he wanted, and so did not write again. Then she'd gotten a Christmas card from Sid. Mary, his wife, must have addressed the envelope, because Betty would have immediately recognized Sid's handwriting. No personal message there, either—just "Joy to the World" and a printed "Sid and Mary Edwards." It had been a bright spot in her first Christmas here in the snug little house she'd bought after being cast out, a woman in her sixties without a family or a life she could call a life.

It still burned her up to think that both she and Sid Senior, two capable, intelligent, hardworking people, could be put out to pasture just like that by a sharp operator like Sid Junior—someone she'd known since he was a boy— just because they were over sixty. Of course, it was harder on Sid Senior to be fired from his own company by his own son, although Betty had always suspected that Emily, Sid's daughter, had probably concurred with her brother's actions. Emmie was a good deal more interested in money than even her brother was. And money was certainly the reason why Junior had taken matters into his own hands. Emmie had never worked for Edwards & Son, although she was an officer of the corporation. Emily Edwards Ruin. Betty never failed to chuckle over the name Emmie had married. It was perfect, since Sid had hinted that Bob Ruin had more than once brought his family to the brink of bankruptcy.

"Don't start with me," Betty said warningly over her shoulder. Tina, the Botero-like, steadfastly ill-tempered cat she'd unwillingly and unwittingly acquired, stalked in from the kitchen, evidently gravely displeased with the lower-priced cat food Betty was trying out on her.

Tina rubbed up against Betty's legs, but Betty wasn't fooled for a second that there was true affection involved. Tina sat expectantly beside the closed front door.

"Go out, then," Betty said, and opened the door, "but don't play in the traffic." Not that Timberhill Road was heavily traveled, especially not in winter.

Tina twitched her tail and proceeded out the front door in a stately manner as befitted her matronly figure.

Betty looked at the FedEx envelope she still clutched, frowned, and pulled the tab to open it.

There was a white business envelope inside with her name and address neatly typed, and the return address of Edwards & Son in the corner. She held the letter up to the light. From years of managing the Edwards & Son office, she was pretty good at detecting letters that might contain checks—not that she expected a check from anyone. She determined that the envelope held a single typewritten sheet, no other enclosures.

She opened it and glanced at the bottom of the letter. It was signed by Sid Junior.

"Dear Betty:

"I hope you have been enjoying your retirement. We have been very active here, and certainly miss your smiling face."

That stretched the truth, Betty thought. She was definitely gone, and her smiling face long forgotten.

"I'm afraid I have some bad news," the letter went on. "You may not have heard that Dad suffered a stroke a few weeks before Christmas."

Betty felt a sudden tightness in her chest. Poor Sid.

That explained the lack of a personal message from him on her Christmas card. She'd believed his silence meant that he'd chosen to erase their past together from his memory. Of course, Mary wouldn't dream of mentioning Sid's illness, that was personal business, not to be shared with a mere employee. Old-fashioned Yankee that she was, Mary followed the accepted pattern. Even if your husband was dreadfully ill, you still sent cards at Christmas. She read on.

"Dad's speech and physical functions were damaged, and Mother wasn't up to caring for him properly in a strange place, so she decided to bring him back home to Connecticut. They're settled in with us in Wethersfield for however long it takes."

She understood "however long." He'd been brought home to die. Poor Sid.

Wendy, Sid Junior's wife, wouldn't be pleased with this turn of events. A sick old man living out his days in her glamorous white colonial mansion high on a hill. The house had been the Seniors' home until his retirement. Emmie had wanted the place, but Junior had been too clever for his sister. He'd snagged the house—reportedly a "loan" from his parents—as well as the business.

"However, I'm glad to report that he has shown marked improvement through his therapy, and the doctors say he could live for several years."

Years! Wendy must be fit to be tied, Betty thought. And the grandchildren . . . She doubted that those two spoiled teenagers would relish the idea of an infirm grandfather and a difficult grandmother in their midst for years—any more than their mother would.

"He is not up to receiving visitors," Sid Junior went on

to say, quashing Betty's impulse to drive up to the Hartford area, a fairly short trip from her new home here in East Moulton, Connecticut, to see him. "However, there is one matter in which you could be of assistance to him and the company, for old times' sake. As you may recall, when Dad decided to retire . . ." Betty gazed out the window. "Decided to retire," indeed.

Outside, she could see Tina crouching beneath the branches of a low, decorative evergreen bush, pretending to gear up to stalk some bit of wildlife, even though few small animals were yet convinced that a warmish day meant that spring was anywhere near arriving. Besides, Tina's mere presence during the past couple of months had effectively driven the birds across the fields to the amply filled bird feeders at the house of her neighbor, Penny Saks. Tina chose to ignore reality as much as Sid Junior.

". . . decided to retire, we chose to keep his office as he had left it, in case he ever wanted to come back to the firm. Now we feel certain that he will not be able to manage even a visit, and as we are expanding the company, we are in desperate need of the office space. I intend to clear his office as soon as possible. It is my hope—and my father's—that you will agree to undertake the task. With your long experience with the company, he agrees that you would be best suited to determine what material from his files should be retained. Naturally, we will pay you for your time."

The files. Oh, yes. She remembered them well. A long row of five-drawer metal filing cabinets crammed with correspondence, technical material, accounting records, folders neatly labeled according to a system Sid Senior had devised—and only Betty really understood—so that either of them could put their hands on anything in seconds.

Sid had been so particular about his things. For a moment, Betty recalled minor differences of opinion about where certain papers should be filed. Sid had always won out. "Don't want the boy to be messing around," he'd said more than once. "None of his business." And the filing system grew more complicated—to foil any attempt by Siddie to figure it out.

Junior, of course, hadn't dared to toss the files as soon as his father left for his Arizona retirement, since he might have shown up again at any time, furious to discover that his files had been emptied or changed. He'd always had the power to send Junior cowering before his anger, until Junior had won the final round and seen that his father was sent off to the desert. So the remote possibility of Senior's return had vanished with his illness, and Junior was no longer under his father's thumb.

Now Junior was actually inviting her back, even though their parting had not been cordial. Both Junior and his sister Emmie deeply resented Sid Senior's private arrangements to insure Betty's financial well-being. She looked back at the paragraph she had just read. "My hope—and my father's. . . . he agrees . . ."

How had Sid Senior expressed his desire that Betty handle the clearing up of his office if his speech was impaired?

Then it came to her, and she wanted to believe that it was the right answer. Sid Senior had always been meticulous about planning ahead. The discussion of Betty's possible role, and the agreement, must have taken place before his illness. He had indicated to Junior what he wanted her to do, well before death was standing at his side. The long years—and more—that they had shared had not been forgotten, after all. He still trusted her. The thought brought her a little peace, which was quickly overtaken by concern. She had to see him, see what damage had been done, help him. Yet that would probably be denied her. He didn't need her now. He had his wife, his family.

"It may be possible," Junior wrote in conclusion, "for you to visit Dad later, when he's having one of his good days, since you'll be here at the company working on the office."

I'm an old fool, Betty thought, and Junior's the smart one. He knows I'd jump at the chance to see Sid—on the condition that I agree to be around doing chores for the office. She put the letter from Junior under the mantel clock she'd received from Edwards & Son the day she retired.

She'd stay with her friends Cora and Dave Welles at their place in the apartment complex near Hartford, where she'd lived before she'd retired and moved south to East Moulton. They'd been begging her to visit, but in the six months she'd lived in this pleasant small town she hadn't felt like stepping back into the old days, as she'd tried to construct a new life for herself with temp work and community activities.

Betty watched Tina for a minute, as she gathered courage to dial the familiar number of the offices of Edwards & Son, in the old-fashioned, redbrick building on the outskirts of Hartford.

She didn't recognize the receptionist's voice when the

phone was finally answered. "This is Betty Trenka. May I speak with Mr. Edwards?"

Obviously the young woman had never heard of Betty Trenka. How soon they had forgotten—or rather, how quickly the staff turned over. Miriam Kozelski had been a gem at the receptionist's job, and seemed destined to stay in it forever. Had Junior gotten rid of her, too?

"Mr. Edwards is on another call. May I take a message?"

Betty had to spell Trenka and assure the young woman that Mr. Edwards would know what the call was about. "My company?" Betty thought for a minute. "Edwards and Son," she said.

"Yeah, right. Look, ma'am. I don't have time for jokes, what with the stuff going on around here." She sounded harried.

"Really," Betty said, more kindly. "I used to work there." She left her number and went out to the kitchen. Tina had worked her way around to the backyard and was lurking near the back door. Betty was beginning to feel a little apprehensive about her coming task at the company, but the idea of Sid Senior incapacitated and perhaps in pain upset her. She had been tied so closely to him, and to Edwards & Son. The pain of the break from both had finally begun to heal, and now this.

Death . . . She wasn't young herself, with sixty-four staring her in the face, but at least she still had her health. But unlike Sid, she was entirely alone, except for her cousin, Sister Rita, who served the poor, the battered, and the homeless in Boston—and one difficult cat who didn't generally behave as though she actually thought she belonged with Betty.

She did have some new friends. Her neighbor across Timberhill Road, Ted Kelso, was certainly a supportive friend. He knew all about computers, so he had helped her upgrade the system she used for her occasional typing jobs. He'd even been urging her to sign up with one of the online services, so she could sit at her computer and communicate with people all over the world.

"Explore the Internet," he kept saying. "Get into a chat group. You'll never be lonely."

She wasn't lonely now, and she wasn't convinced that electronic messages on her screen were the answer as she struggled to find a comfortable structure for her life, the way she'd had structure and purpose for all those years before they were snatched away. She knew she needed a real focus for her life, and she'd been thinking about it, but nothing grabbed her attention the way working for Sid at Edwards & Son had.

She tried to imagine Sid Senior without speech. He'd been a man who loved to talk, about anything and everything. Politics, books, business, sports. What he'd seen on television, in movies; world events, places he and Mary had visited.

She felt tears welling up, and that was not acceptable. She resolutely put her coming adventure and Sid's condition out of her mind. She had work to do. She was typing up a résumé for a young woman from East Moulton who had dreams of leaving small-town life and making it big in New York City. She'd seen the notice Betty had posted on the community bulletin board in the East Moulton supermarket, offering reasonable typing and office services. Her rates were modest, but at least it gave her something to do.

Miss Levenger was what she assumed would be called "Generation X," a graduate of the state university, with no pronounced social skills or personality. Apparently her career goal was an entry-level vice presidency, and she expected Betty not only to type her résumé but to structure it to make her modest achievements sound marketable.

A pity, Betty thought, that Miss Levenger was incapable of typing it herself, or of understanding where she probably stood in the general scheme of business things. Somewhere a bit farther down the corporate ladder than vice president. She'd learn the realities soon enough.

Sid Junior returned her call at eleven. The false geniality didn't fool her for a second.

"Of course I'll be glad to help out, Sid," she said. "When would be convenient?"

When he said, "Monday," she was taken aback. So soon? "Emmie will be in town with the old Ruin." He laughed at his own joke. He and Bob Ruin had never gotten along.

"I can arrange it," Betty said. "Yes, it will be interesting to see the old place again. Changes? I imagine there have been many." Then she asked cautiously, "How is your father doing?"

"As well as can be expected," Junior said curtly. "He seems to think he'll be able to come back to the office. That's why I want everything gone from his old office, so he'll have no reason to start showing up if he's ever able to. Not that he can get about at all just yet, but there's a chance for improvement, if another stroke doesn't get him." Sid Junior stopped for a moment, perhaps contemplating the possibility of a final solution. "It's been hell on Mother, on all of us, but he keeps hanging on." Sid didn't sound too happy at the thought. "He should go to a nursing home, where he'd be among people like himself, but Mother can't make up her mind to do it."

Sid would hate the idea of a nursing home. That really *would* kill him.

"Wendy and the kids are finding it terribly difficult . . ." Sid Junior paused again, and Betty knew that something else was coming. "Betty, maybe while you're up here, you can talk to Mother, convince her that a nursing home would be best for him. You could certainly convince him. He always listened to you."

Yes, he did, Betty thought, but no, I will not become involved in the Edwardses' personal business. Mary Edwards certainly does not want to listen to me, and I don't necessarily agree that a nursing home is the answer. Betty knew the real answer. She should be caring for Sid patiently—as she had cared for him through all their years at the company.

"We'll discuss it when I get there," Betty said. "On Monday. Maybe I'll have a chance to talk to him. I can stay until Wednesday."

"Good," Junior said. "Having him around at home all the time, knowing he understands everything, even if he can't speak, is holding me back from what I want to do. A nursing home would be the ideal solution. I hope you'll do what you can to persuade . . . everyone."

Junior's ideal solution, Betty realized sadly, was to see his father dead. An old man who was only in the way.

CHAPTER 2

BETTY FINISHED Miss Levenger's résumé around noon. It looked nice and professional, but she wondered whether Miss Levenger's summer job as a checkout cashier at the East Moulton supermarket would have much of an impact on the personnel director of a major corporation. Well, it showed she was willing to work, and she could probably make change. (The supermarket cash registers were still the old-fashioned kind that gave a total but no electronic calculation of change to be returned for the money tendered.) At worst, she probably knew the price of a half gallon of milk. She'd taken some marketing courses at the university, and she'd majored in history, had graduated with honors. Betty had to admit that she was pretty, sexy even, the kind of young woman who brightens up an office.

Betty shook her head. She remembered walking into the offices of Edwards & Son for the first time all those years ago, barely out of her teens, with a handful of secretarial skills and perhaps a little common sense. Awkward and certainly neither pretty nor sexy, even in the terms of the 1950s and 1960s. Not then and not now. She was always too tall, with thick glasses and a heavy braid piled on top of her head.

She'd been scared that day, applying for her first job and about to be interviewed by the president of the company.

The first person she'd encountered, after the receptionist who put her in the cold, dim conference room, had been old Arnie Harris, the bookkeeper, a big man with a genial smile, shaggy hair, and a tie that was always loosened.

"I'm Arnie Harris. Bookkeeper here. You the new kid?"

"Not yet," she said. "I'm Elizabeth Trenka. Mr. Edwards is interviewing me for the job."

"He's a cupcake. And a mensch. You'll do fine, Betty."

She'd lost her nervousness in wondering if she would ever persuade people to call her Elizabeth, not Betty. She'd been trying all her life, and she failed with Arnie as well as almost everyone else. But she forgave Arnie, who turned out to be a treasure, someone who'd loved numbers, cared about balancing the checkbook, saw to it that the tax forms were meticulously prepared, the ledgers all in order.

As her responsibilities increased over the years, she'd come to rely on old Arnie for sensible advice and the assurance that even in the midst of a crisis, everything would work out all right. Sid had been close to Arnie, too. As she understood it, Arnie took care of Sid's personal financial business, balancing his checkbook and even paying his bills under some private arrangement.

Of course, Arnie wasn't old then, in his forties maybe—close to the age Sid Junior was now—but for thirty-seven years, she and Arnie had grown older together at Edwards & Son. It seemed unlikely that he was still with the company, if he was even alive. On the other hand, although he was older than she by fifteen years or so, he hadn't been asked to retire when she and Senior were given their walking papers. Sid Junior probably found him too valuable to get rid of.

It turned out that Arnie had been the last person she'd seen at Edwards & Son, just as he'd been the first.

"You'll be okay, Betty," he'd said as she lugged her clock out to the parking lot. "I told you way back when that the job would work out for you, and look at you, going strong a hundred years later. It's Sid I worry about. It's hard on us old men when the Young Turks start thinking they know a better way." He shook his head. "And playing golf out there in the desert sun can't be good for a man of his age."

Betty looked over Miss Levenger's résumé in case she'd mistyped something. She hated the spellchecker, believing that a well-trained person knew how to spell. Still, errors had a way of creeping in, especially lately with the touch of stiffness in her fingers. She worried that arthritis might be setting in.

Arnie had helped her carry the clock, and then he'd said, "You drop around to see me and Sophie if you get bored," and had added something she'd never understood, and she'd forgotten it until now. "My advice, Betty, is to look under *K* when things turn bad."

"I don't understand."

"You don't need to now. But someday. Remember, *K* is the key." Arnie had winked and given her a brief hug, not something he was known to do freely. And Betty had driven away forever, almost, from the job that had worked out for her, with her retirement clock resting on the front seat of her car.

Sid Senior (a remarkably handsome man, she'd thought

from the first moment) had interviewed her in the conference room, explaining that Edwards & Son had been a
small company, manufacturing locks and related hardware—an old Connecticut tradition—but it had grown
markedly during the war with a lot of defense contracts,
and afterward, it found markets not only across the United
States but overseas as well.

Like Betty, Sid was tall, and people said he bore a resemblance to Franchot Tone, a movie star she'd long ad-
mired in her weekly forays to the local movie house. She
came to believe in the resemblance, but at the interview
she nodded at his remarks and hoped that she didn't appear too stupid and inept to be hired. After all, she'd not
had any experience, although she'd done well at the secretarial school she'd attended against her father's wishes.
Pa had been so traditional about a woman's place, but
she'd defied him to educate herself a bit and find work.

She'd never believed she'd find her prince and settle
down the way Pa expected her to. Ma hinted she should
consider a religious vocation, but Cousin Rita had taken
that path and had convinced Betty that the degree of faith
required was not in her.

"We've got more salesmen now, more secretaries, more
vice presidents than I can keep track of," Mr. Edwards
said. He didn't become "Sid" to her for several months. "I
need a right-hand person, someone to handle all kinds of
matters, administer the office, oversee everything. Not a
secretary. I have one of those, but she's not right for what I
have in mind. Not an administrative assistant. I don't want
a yes-woman. I want an office manager, a person who'll
learn all the ropes, understand how I want the company to
work, someone I can trust completely. I'm going to be

bringing my son into the business in a few years, when he's finished college, but I'd like to think someone besides me knows what I want right now. Think you can do it?"

"I believe I'm a fast learner," Betty said primly, "and I'm organized. My mother says I have good common sense. I can type and make telephone calls. I . . ." She hesitated. "I'm tall enough to intimidate short women and short men if necessary, and the taller ones can look me in the eye."

Sid laughed, a nice warm laugh.

"And you can trust me. I really want a job."

"You have it," Sid said.

By the time Betty left, after three-plus decades, Edwards & Son was beginning to shrink back to the size of the old days, before the war. The salesmen were lured away by companies that promised better commissions, the secretaries weren't needed and were let go, vice presidents were erased from the letterhead. The competition was making business difficult.

After Betty had been with the firm for over a decade, Sid Junior was brought in when he'd finished college and spent some time bumming around the country, spending his father's money. Junior gradually got enough power to start downsizing seriously last year, beginning with his father and Betty. He claimed that new electronic locks were ruining the market for Edwards's old standard locks with metal keys, yet even in the face of competition, he hadn't done much to change anything. Senior had discussed the future with Betty, but not with Junior, and was in the process of planning a new direction for the company, using new technical discoveries to create better locks. All those plans were somewhere in the files Junior wanted her to clear out.

Finally, about a year ago, the pressure to get Senior to retire had started in earnest. An insidious campaign, in Betty's opinion. Sid Junior would ask his father for documents that had been mysteriously misplaced. (That reflected on Betty, too. She had never misplaced anything in her life.) He'd claim that important phone calls weren't being returned, but Betty was certain he'd never been given the messages. He claimed that Senior spent too much time away from the office playing golf, that he needed to take it easier.

After the day she'd discovered Junior purposely putting an important contract in the wrong file, Betty decided never to trust him again, but it had always been clear to Betty that his father trusted her far more than he trusted his son.

"Arnie, what's up with Junior?" she'd once asked the bookkeeper.

"Different generations. Siddie thinks he'd make a lot more money with his father gone. With his mother and sister, he controls the majority of the stock, and he wants to be boss. He could skim off what he could and put nothing back. Drive the place into the ground. Or sell it for the best offer. There have been some lately. The sister would go along with that. The Ruin guy she married has a gambling problem, and they always need money. Senior's bailed him out more than once, but don't worry, big Sid isn't going to let anything happen to Edwards & Son, not while he's in charge." But Sid wasn't really in charge now.

Back then, Emily would show up from her home in

Westport and nag her father about retiring. His wife, Mary, never talked much to Betty, but one day even she'd said she wished Sid would slow down and spend more time with her, with the grandchildren, travel a bit more.

"I worry about him, Betty," she said once. "He does too much. Junior could handle the business, but Sid won't hear of it. It's his life. At least he has you." There was no trace of rancor, but Betty understood that Mary didn't like her, although she was always civil.

Finally, they'd worn Senior down, so the day that Junior told his father that the board (Mary, Siddie, and Emmie, and a couple of Junior's pals) wanted him out and Siddie in, Sid had gone unexpectedly quietly. She remembered his face when he told her. It was right after Siddie had told her that her services would no longer be required by Edwards & Son.

Betty didn't want to dwell on the past any longer, so she called Cora Welles, who was delighted to have Betty spend a few days with her in Hartford.

"I'll come up on Sunday afternoon," Betty said, "and stay until Wednesday. How long can it take to clear out an office?" But she remembered again the crammed filing cabinets. She guessed she'd have to look at every drawer, every folder, but except for the business plans Sid had drawn up, surely there was nothing much that needed to be saved. Two days would certainly do it. "If I won't be too much trouble."

"Stay as long as you like," Cora said. "Dave is getting tired of talking to me. It will do him good to have a new face to look at, and new ears to listen. And a decent card-player across the table." David Welles himself had been

retired for a couple of years. He was a fixer-upper, a tin-
kerer with broken appliances, so he always kept busy.
And then, the two of them were always on the road, visiting their children and relatives across the country. Betty
had taken the Welleses as an example of what retirement
should be like. It hadn't worked that way for her, but . . .
Tina marched in and jumped up onto the telephone table.

"What am I going to do with you while I'm away?"
Betty asked. "And get down. Now."

Tina looked at her briefly but warily. Obedience was
not one of her strong points.

"Shoo," Betty said hopefully. Tina blinked and moved
away from the phone. Betty called Ted Kelso across the
street. "I wonder if I could drop by for a couple of minutes. I need to ask a favor."

"Can it wait until dinner? I'm finishing a report that I
have to send off this afternoon," Ted said. Ted was a con-
sultant of sorts, although what he consulted on he'd
never explained to her. "I'll cook us something wonder-
ful. Let's make it early, say six o'clock."

"All right," Betty said. Ted's dinner would certainly
be better than a melted-down, prepackaged entrée from
her freezer.

"Elizabeth," Ted said, "you're not sounding your usual
cheerful self. Is it about that damned cat?"

"In a way. But there's more." If anyone would understand about Sid, immobilized as well as speech-impaired
by a stroke, Ted would.

"We'll fix everything up, don't worry. And you don't
need to bring anything."

They had both come to terms with the fact that Betty
was not gifted with any culinary talent, or even with a

good eye for buying the ideal accompaniment to a meal, although to her credit, she'd had one or two minor successes. For a time, Ted's ability to whip up gourmet meals out of practically nothing had made her feel depressed about her domestic deficiencies. But then Ted had pointed out that it was more a lack of personal inclination than an inherent inadequacy, and she had felt better. She was definitely an undomesticated person, and not everyone could be like her other neighbor, Penny Saks, who devoted her considerable energies to feeding, clothing, and cleaning up after a husband and three rambunctious blond boys, not to mention doing handicrafts galore. Betty thought of her as a true heroine of the hot glue gun set.

"I need to drive into town," Betty said. "Can I get you anything?"

"Nothing I can think of. Federal Express is picking up my report," Ted said. "When I saw the FedEx truck this morning, I thought they'd come too early, but it was for you. Well, you'll tell me about what you received when I see you later."

In quiet East Moulton, and on even quieter Timberhill Road, there were few secrets.

Miss Levenger's résumé was ready to be picked up that afternoon, so Betty decided to take a couple of her office outfits, unworn for six months, to the dry cleaner's, to be ready for her return to Edwards & Son.

The Buick hummed to life promptly. Unlike the local wildlife, but rather like Tina, it had been fooled into thinking warmish February meant spring, in spite of a light snow that had fallen last week and had already melted away in her yard. No grumpy engine turnover against the cold. As Betty backed out onto Timberhill Road, she remembered an old saying in the upstate Connecticut town where she'd grown up. Green February, green graves? How did it go? Something about unseasonable weather meaning unseasonable dying. She wondered if it was a Yankee saying, or something her Czech grandparents had brought over from the old country, a tattered remnant of the Austro-Hungarian Empire.

As she drove along the smooth, curving road toward the town center, she thought again of Sid Senior, and this time, tears did gather in her eyes. She didn't know a good deal about strokes, but she seemed to recall that even when speech and movement were damaged, the mind continued to work quite well. How could Sid manage with his communication shut down? Mary wouldn't have the patience to try to understand him, nor would Wendy or the kids.

I would understand what he was trying to say, she thought. I always knew what he was thinking before he said a word. It used to drive him crazy, but other people thought it was magic.

CHAPTER 3

EAST MOULTON was never crowded, even in the summer months when tourists on the way south to the shores of Long Island Sound passed through, plundering the scattered antique stores and gawking at the picture-perfect New England village, complete with town green, white Congregational church, and nineteenth-century Victorian houses. Today Main Street seemed especially empty. The kids were in school, and most people did their shopping out at the mall on the highway. But Betty's mind was not on the traffic lights blinking green, yellow, red, or the occasional piles of dirty, melting snow left over from last week's sudden storm. She was thinking of those crammed filing cabinets in Sid's office, his big desk, and the comfortable battered leather chair behind it. Sid had never been one for fancy offices. "The quality of a company is the quality of its goods and its people," he used to say, "not its office furniture."

Hmm. With Junior in charge now, she was sure his office was an executive's dream. Wendy would have seen to that.

She was briefly tempted to stop at Perkins pharmacy to ask Molly or Perk, her husband, the pharmacist, about strokes, but decided against it. Molly was the font of all gossip, and Lord knew what tales would get spread around town if she asked questions about strokes. Her own doctor was a better source of information. She'd call him, or maybe she'd find a book.

There was a big Barnes & Noble store in the mall. But what was there to know? It hit you; it left you disabled to a greater or lesser degree. She seemed to recall, though, that stroke victims were likely to suffer another one sooner or later. She hoped Sid would hang on long enough for her to see him one more time, rather than die promptly to please his son.

Instead of heading right along Main Street to Dwyer's Dry Cleaners, Betty made a sudden right turn onto a quiet residential street, drove two blocks, and pulled into the parking lot of St. Jude's. The squat, redbrick church couldn't compete aesthetically with the elegant, white-steepled Congregational church. Betty had set foot in it only once since she'd moved to East Moulton, but she had not been moved to reestablish links with the Church. She wasn't sure why she was here now, except that some old remnants of the faith of her upbringing were encouraging her to find solace to ease her aching sorrow.

She hesitated as she entered the darkened church, seeing along the sides of the nave a flutter of bright dots of light from the votive candles that had been lighted by the faithful. There was no one visible, no prayerful figures, no priest near the altar, although the colors of the narrow stained-glass windows glowed from the outside sun. Betty walked along the right side of the nave, looking at the alcoves that harbored statues of a few saints, and stopped before St. Jude, who held pride of place because it was his church. The saint of Impossible Causes. She remembered that well, and her mother's novenas when troubles came upon the family. None of the stubby white candles in the rack were lighted, so she dug out a couple of quarters, dropped them into the metal box, and was startled by how loud a sound they made as they clunked to the bottom. When she was young, you could actually light a votive with a taper, but now an electrical switch turned on the candles.

The flame on a votive at St. Jude's feet sputtered and then burned steadily, and all the while she whispered Sid's name and a confused sort of prayer for his recovery. She wasn't sure one should offer prayers to a deity and his saints if the faith they represented was no longer professed, or more to the point in her case, if one felt beyond that faith's boundaries. She sat in a nearby pew for a few minutes, smelling the hot candle wax and the memory of incense, imagining the sound of the Latin of the Mass as she had known it, and feeling a kind of peace creeping through her troubled spirit. At least she had always tried to be a good person.

The day seemed colder when she emerged from the church and drove back to Main Street. She parked in front of Dwyer's Dry Cleaners.

"Can I get these things back by Friday or Saturday, Mr. Dwyer?"

"Sure, Miz Trenka. You goin' travelin'?"

Ed Dwyer liked to play the crusty old-timer, but he was really just as nosy as Molly at the pharmacy.

Betty hesitated. Whatever she said would promptly be passed on to Molly, and the rest of the town.

"I have some business out of town," she said. "I

thought I ought to look professional." As it was, the town saw her mostly in long denim skirts and her hooded plaid jacket, sensible shoes, with boots and jeans when the weather turned bad. "You know how these corporate executives are." She couldn't resist a little self-promotion.

"Got yourself some work, have you? That's good. Keeps a body young to have plenty to do. I don't care for this unseasonably warm weather, though. Gets the bulbs all confused, if you know what I mean. But I hear a weather front is moving in; might bring more snow." Ed handed her a receipt for her clothes. He'd marked them down for Friday. "To tell the truth, I could do without the snow."

"I'll see you Friday," Betty said. "I've got to get home to my cat."

As if Tina cared. Ed would talk all day if given the chance, and Betty had things to do. For one thing, she'd have to tell the librarian that she wouldn't be around to volunteer at the library next Wednesday. She wondered if she could find a replacement who would please the librarian, not always an easy achievement. Frankly, Betty didn't care if Patricia Cornwell and John Grisham got reshelved promptly. But for the librarian it was a matter of life and death. Betty sat in the Buick for a few minutes thinking.

Betty held to old-fashioned principles: If you were invited to dinner, you did not come empty-handed. But considering the number of meals Ted had provided, she was beginning to run out of ideas, having used up very good wine, very good pastries from Nilsson's bakery, even a tiny amount of beluga caviar she'd bought on a visit to New Haven. East Moulton didn't hold out the promise of many such delicacies. In any case, she was expressly forbidden to bring food.

As she sat in her car outside of Dwyer's, an idea began to develop. Along one of the several country roads leading from East Moulton to the highway were a number of farms with roadside stands, which in the recent autumn had displayed arrays of homegrown produce: pumpkins, squash, baskets of apples, even green tomatoes. She remembered one stand that sat in front of a long greenhouse. She'd never stopped to inquire about the greenhouse, but it seemed to promise flowers, and flowers were the answer to her problem.

Even though she'd seen Ted's carefully nurtured garden behind his low stone house, planted largely for his bees, by now there would be nothing blooming—and nothing likely to bloom for months. She imagined the proprietor of the produce stand probably grew flats of pansies and petunias, lobelias and impatiens to sell to summer-weekend gardeners in East Moulton. So, likely nothing fancy, but surely something to carry across at dinnertime.

She drove away from the town center and in a few minutes pulled into the dirt parking area in front of the house with the greenhouse. The produce stand was empty, and the neat white house behind it seemed serenely unoccupied. An apple orchard spread out behind the house, and empty dirt fields where the vegetables grew in the summer. When she got out of the car, she caught sight of a figure moving behind the glass panes of the greenhouse, among an encouraging array of greenery.

There was a door at the near end of the greenhouse, and it opened when she turned the knob. Inside it was damp and warm, far warmer than outside. Rows of fluorescent lights crisscrossed the roof of the greenhouse, and Betty sighed with pleasure at the sight before her. Along the sides was a profusion of orchids in all ranges of purple, yellow, orange, and white. Sprays of tiny purple, red, yellow flowers, and great single blooms, looking like creatures from outer space.

"May I help you?"

Betty tore her eyes away from the orchids and looked around. Then she glanced down. A tiny Japanese woman, quite young-looking, with glossy black hair pulled back behind her ears, was smiling up at Betty. She wore an oversized denim smock and corduroy slacks, heavy work gloves, and thick-soled sandals.

"I'm sorry," Betty said. "The door was open . . ."

"We are not really open for business," the woman said.

A man's voice, old and quavery, called from a distant part of the greenhouse, words that Betty didn't understand. The woman answered, presumably in Japanese.

"My father is asking who is here," the woman said. "He is old and curious. Very old." She sounded sad.

"I'm Betty Trenka. I live here in town and was passing by. I was hoping to find flowers for a friend. Your orchids are beautiful."

The woman bowed slightly. "Thank you. I am Miho, but I am sorry. We grow our orchids for wholesale, and for our own pleasure. We don't really sell to the public. But," she added quickly as Betty frowned, "perhaps I can select something—with my father's permission. He is the orchid expert."

Betty was puzzled. In her months in East Moulton, no one had mentioned a Japanese family living in their midst, and surely that was information that Molly would have enjoyed sharing. "I imagine they are difficult to grow and care for."

Miho smiled. "They can be difficult children," she said. "And like children, they can be expensive—but some of them are happy in the right conditions for a very long time."

Now they were joined by an old man leaning on a cane. He watched Betty with some suspicion as he made his way slowly toward them. Remembering her association with Mr. Mitsui, an executive who had been involved with ZigZag Corporation, the company where she had worked as a temp, Betty bowed to him with what she hoped was the right degree of respect. His suspicion seemed to vanish, and she thought she detected a twitch of a smile. He said something in Japanese.

Miho said, "This is my father, Mr. Takahashi. He is honored to welcome you." She spoke to him, and Betty heard "Betty-san" among her words. The old man tottered to a shelf of pots holding flower spikes with small lavender and white flowers with deeper purple hearts.

"This is a *phalaenopsis*, moth orchid," Miho said. "See, the flowers look like little moths. It behaves well, and these buds will flower in the coming weeks. You will water when the planting medium is dry, feed every two, three weeks, and keep at sixty degrees or above. Keep from sun but give it light. That is all. When the flowers fall, wait a time and then cut just below the last flower on the spike. Very often, it will bloom again. My father says that this is the best one." Miho took the pot from the old man and handed it to Betty. "Twenty-five dollars."

"Surely not," Betty said. "It must be more." She imagined that orchids were very expensive plants.

"A special price for a visitor," Miho said, "who bows to my father with respect."

"Thank you," Betty said. It would more than do for Ted. At least, Miho made it sound simple to care for. "Do you know Ted Kelso?"

"Of course," Miho said. "He often buys plants for his garden here, and vegetables in the summertime. And he brings us honey from his beehives."

"The orchid is for him. Do you think he'll like it?"

"Ted-san likes all growing things," Miho said. "A wise man, and brave, don't you think?"

Brave? He lived his life confined to a wheelchair, with few complaints that Betty had heard. She supposed he was brave. She generally thought of him as quiet about his disabilities, although she knew he harbored anger and bitterness that would break through unexpectedly, often as biting sarcasm.

Betty wondered if poor Sid was as brave, and whether he, too, might like a pretty *phalaenopsis* orchid to brighten his long, silent, and motionless days.

"If Ted has any questions about the care and feeding of the orchid, I'm sure he'll ask you," Betty said. Even Ted had never mentioned Miho and her orchids, although surely he'd viewed this marvelous greenhouse. She felt a sudden flash of chagrin. Perhaps he disliked orchids, and here she was foisting one on him. "Ted is my friend and neighbor."

"There's no better friend," Miho said. "He was my husband's friend as well." Betty noticed the past tense.

Miho wrapped white paper loosely around the pot and

plant and waved as Betty drove back toward town. At least she wasn't bringing Ted sour cream dip, to smooth the way to asking him to care for Tina while she was in Hartford. And she'd ask about Miho, that was for sure.

In the middle of East Moulton, she could bear it no longer. She pulled up in front of the pharmacy and strolled in.

"Ooh-hoo! Betty!" Molly bustled out from the back of the store. "What's this I hear about you getting back into business?"

So soon? Betty wondered if Ed Dwyer had simply gotten on the phone as soon as she'd walked out of the cleaners'.

"Not really," she said. "Just a bit of clearing up at my old company. Molly, why haven't you ever mentioned the Japanese girl with the greenhouse out on the county road?"

"Nothing to mention," Molly said shortly, and without a smile. "She married a local boy who was stationed in Japan after the war."

"Surely she's not old enough!"

"Oh, it was long after the actual war. I'm not sure when . . ."

Betty was sure that Molly was sure about everything, but was being evasive.

"Tom Crandell was a lovely boy," Molly said. "Very popular here in town. Football and good grades, and all the girls loved him. Then he went off to Vietnam, and ended up getting mixed up with foreigners."

"Rather a different war," Betty said. But Miho was definitely Japanese, not Vietnamese. "He must have met her when on leave in Tokyo. She seems a nice person, devoted to her father."

"Humph." Molly busied herself rearranging a shelf of Ace bandages, when no rearrangement appeared necessary.

"Miho spoke of her husband in the past tense," Betty said. "Is he dead?"

"There was some trouble . . ." Molly couldn't find anything else to rearrange. "He left her," Molly said. "Could be dead as well, for all I know. I have no idea where they met. Maybe in Hawaii. As for the father, my brother was killed in the Pacific during World War II. He was the family's pride and joy." Molly stared mournfully into space. "They say the old man was an admiral in the Japanese Navy, so I hold him responsible."

"I don't know how you could know that . . . ," Betty began, but was stopped by the look on Molly's face. "He must be close to a hundred then," Betty said. She sensed that Mr. Takahashi was a subject on which Molly was not likely to expound for substantial minutes. "Amazing, isn't it, to have lived so long and be apparently in such good health?" Poor Sid was a mere seventy, with little hope of reaching Mr. Takahashi's years.

"It's of no interest to me," Molly said. "He can't die soon enough to suit me, after what he put me through . . . what she put Tommy through."

Betty couldn't resist further comment. She'd never convince Molly that Mr. Takahashi wasn't responsible for her brother's death, but she was curious about Miho. "What did she put him through?"

"She had him growing flowers. A fine strapping boy like that, with all kinds of opportunities to make something of himself. There's plenty in town who feel the way

I do, especially Tommy's family. They made him leave her. She's supposed to have been some kind of nurse, but would she work at that? Not her. She had to indulge that father of hers and grow flowers. At least Tommy had the gumption to try farming, do a little work in construction when it turned up. I try never to mention her myself. Pack of foreigners. Don't know enough to stay where they belong."

Betty left the pharmacy shaken. Prejudice was never much a part of her life. Yes, she'd been patronized by the Yankees in her hometown who mocked her Eastern European ancestors, and even her religion, but her family and friends had stuck together and she'd survived. Molly's antagonism seemed pointless. East Moulton didn't seem like such a friendly little town, after all. She was looking forward to getting away to Hartford for a few days, to face her other problems. Another family in turmoil.

CHAPTER 4

MISS LEVENGER had been summoned to appear for her résumé around four, so Betty had an hour until she arrived. She removed the paper from the orchid, so she could admire it as she paid a few bills and thought a bit about the old days, when she and Sid, along with Arnie at the adding machine, Miriam at the front desk, and a handful of salesmen had made the company go. Even Bob Ruin, Emmie's husband, had worked there for a time right after they were married, and there was the good-looking boy who used to run errands for Junior and act as his "chauffeur" when called upon. She couldn't remember his name, something odd. The factory had practically run itself. Fortunately Junior preferred taking clients to lunch and "traveling on business" to working in the office, so he never troubled them much until he got the idea that he should be president.

Business had been good, as was her time with Sid. There were hardware conventions, where Betty had worked at the company's exhibit booth with Sid and Junior, and had even gone to some of the cocktail parties and dinners, not always happily. She was not much for social events. She'd made some friends among their competitors, although she hadn't kept in touch with any of them.

The phone rang at three-thirty, and Betty wondered if Miss Levenger had found an excuse not to drive the mile from her family's large faux Tudor home to Betty's house. As she answered, she saw the Federal Express truck arrive at Ted's house across the street to pick up Ted's report.

"Hello, Betty?" A woman's voice, but mature, definitely not Kathy Levenger. "It's Emmie. Emmie Ruin."

Betty was taken aback and fumbled for a reply.

"Sid Edwards's daughter . . ."

"Of course, I remember you, Emmie," Betty said. "I was just surprised to hear from you."

"Siddie says you're coming to the office to do some work," Emmie said.

"I made some arrangements," Betty said. "And I was hoping to see your father while I was there if he's able."

"Oh, I don't think he will be," Emmie said. "Since we've been in town seeing about some business, I've been going over to read to him, but Mother doesn't encourage visitors. Wendy doesn't, either. She spends most of her time tucked away in the little television room watching those ghastly daytime talk shows. I think she'd really like to be featured on the one about 'My father-in-law is driving me crazy.' Or else get the old man completely out of her hair."

Betty's heart sank. More pressure to send Sid off to the nursing home. She hoped Emmie hadn't called her to help persuade him to go.

"What can I do for you, Emmie?"

"Well, you see . . ." Emmie sounded uncertain. "Since

you're coming up here, I was wondering . . . Well, when exactly are you coming?"

"I'll be at the firm at nine on Monday."

"Good. Bob and I are staying until Thursday. Mother needs the help, and I can take her out a bit so she's not cooped up with him all day. And you'll be clearing Dad's files?" She didn't wait for an answer. "The thing is, he has some of my stuff from when I was a kid in the files. You know, report cards and things. I haven't been able to track them down in the stuff he has stored at the house. My brother has refused to let me look at Dad's files on my own, so I was wondering if you'd let me look with you."

She sounded rather more nervous than old report cards would account for. "Of course, Emmie. We'll work something out when I get there. I really have no idea how big a job it's going to be, although I recall the files well."

"I just don't want my brother getting his hands on my private stuff," Emmie said, rather belligerently. "He's been behaving so badly, and I'm worried about Dad . . ." She stopped. "I'll see you on Monday then."

Betty gazed at the orchid thoughtfully. Now what was that all about? And how has Sid Junior been behaving badly? Emily must talk to Junior sometimes, if she already knew that Betty was on her way. She remembered the two of them as children, comparatively speaking, and not getting along all that well then. Emmie was perhaps three or four years younger than Sid, and both of them rather a handful, but she had sort of liked the young Emmie. She remembered her wedding, a truly splendid occasion, but, of course, Mary knew how to arrange something like that to perfection.

At four o'clock, the bell on the front door rang once, twice. Miss Levenger.

"The résumé looks good, I think," Betty said as the luscious Miss Levenger trailed her into the living room and into the small dining room where Betty kept her computer and printer.

"How sweet!" Miss Levenger was an enthusiastic exclaimer. Betty turned to see her gazing at the orchid. She knew it couldn't be Tina, who was a fine figure of a cat, but scarcely sweet.

"It is pretty, isn't it?" Betty said. "I bought it for a friend, but I'm tempted to keep it, or get one for myself. I understand orchids can be a problem, but they do brighten up a room. I'm not good with plants and things like that, so any I acquired would be at risk. Here we are." She handed Miss Levenger a neat pile of résumés. "I only printed ten, so if you want to make any changes, I can easily do so and print more."

"I wouldn't know what to change," Miss Levenger said as she scanned the first page. "Oh! Do you really think I have good communications skills?"

"It doesn't hurt to say so," Betty said. "In my opinion, you don't really have much breadth of experience, so you're selling yourself rather than learned skills."

"I have an interview next week. In Hartford. Not my first choice, but you have to start somewhere. A friend fixed it up with a company where he knows somebody. I'm sooo nervous."

"Show up on time; don't wear clothes that are too flashy." At the moment, Miss Levenger was wearing a minuscule red skirt, black tights, a fluffy red fake fur jacket, and red boots with very high heels. The heels were gold. "Or too much makeup. Be polite, don't smoke. Write a thank-you note after the interview."

"Oh, I don't smoke," Miss Levenger said, with mild horror, and made it sound as though they were talking about indulging in cannibalism or interspecies sex. "What would I say? In the thank-you note, I mean."

"How good of them to take the time to see you, how interesting the job sounds. Anything so they'll remember you as a polite, businesslike person when they make a decision."

"You're so smart, Miss Trenka. Should I be writing this down?"

"It wouldn't hurt," Betty said, and handed her a pencil, nicely sharpened, and a couple of sheets of paper. Miss Levenger dutifully concentrated on writing down what Betty had said, causing Betty to wonder if Miss Levenger would handle the world of business by writing everything down. Well, it couldn't hurt.

"Remember that working in business means that you have to show up pretty much on time and do what you're told to do. The point of that is to make money for the company. Then you get paid, and you can eat, pay for a place to live, and buy nice clothes. It's a simple equation."

She was also not surprised to see Miss Levenger puzzling out Betty's advice, as if she'd never heard of such a thing. Maybe she never had. The Levengers were a fairly well-to-do East Moulton family, if Molly Perkins was to be believed, with Harold Levenger the town's premier, indeed only, attorney. Miss Levenger had probably never made the connection between her father's long hours at his office and the flow of chips, diet Pepsi, sirloin, and shrimp to the family table—and the shopping bags full of cute outfits from The Gap up at the mall, and from Bloomingdale's and Saks from frequent visits to New York.

Betty caught herself as she sank into mean-spirited cynicism over the state of today's youngsters. Miss Levenger would learn, all too soon.

"Miss Trenka, do you think I have any chance at all of getting a job in New York? That's where I really want to go. I mean, like, I don't know a whole lot, not like you do."

"Well . . ." Betty remembered the résumé. "You do know something about computers. That's different from when I started out. Computers hadn't even been invented then. You had to know how to type on an old-fashioned manual typewriter—we didn't even have electric typewriters. I remember when they first came in, we were so excited. And we had to make carbon copies of everything because we didn't have copiers. Sometimes it was four or five carbons, and if we made a typing mistake, we'd have to go back and correct every page."

Miss Levenger's eyes were beginning to glaze.

"You run along now," Betty said, "and remember what I told you. Present yourself as the nice young lady you are. But don't expect to be hired on the first interview, and don't be too disappointed when you're not. It could take a while."

"Daddy wanted me to go to law school," Miss Levenger said. "My grades were good enough, but ick. It's too boring for words. I mean, I know what kind of work he has to do with real estate and wills, and representing kids who get caught knocking down mailboxes and smoking dope. He had an attempted-murder case once, though.

That was sort of interesting. And the guy was really cute."

"Really?" Betty herself had had some little experience with murders, but no "really cute" guys had been party to them.

Miss Levenger continued to fling herself into her employment dreams. "I figure I could find a super job in New York and get a nice apartment. Then I could go out to the clubs you read about and meet fab people. You know, like, have fun."

"It's not all fun," Betty said, suspecting she was sounding like a cautious and boring old biddy. "Work is just what it says: work. And there are a lot of young women competing for the . . . um . . . super jobs."

"I'm going to get the Sunday *New York Times* this week. Mrs. Perkins carries it at the pharmacy, and I told her to save me a copy. It has pages and pages of Help Wanted. I'll just send off my pretty new résumé to simply everyone. I'd love to get into publishing. *Harper's Bazaar* or *Vogue* or *Vanity Fair*. People say I have a good sense of style. Or one of the glam-book publishers, where you run into people like Norman Nailer—"

"Mailer," Betty said.

"Whatever." Now Miss Levenger radiated confidence, or perhaps it was enthusiasm for the potential joys of city living.

"Good luck," Betty said. She slipped the pile of résumés into a manila envelope. "What was it you mentioned about a murder?"

"Oh, Tommy Crandell, one of the guys from town, was accused of trying to kill his wife's father, and maybe even his wife. He wanted to build houses or something on the land, but the old man refused to let him do it. He's Japanese, you know, and really old, so he's not really with it, like, the way things are done in America. My father lost the case, and Tommy went to jail, but just for a little while. And the old guy is still alive, so it all worked out."

"I guess it did," Betty said. "Be sure to let me know how things work out for you."

"I will," Miss Levenger said. "You've been a really, really terrific help. Oh, wait." She fumbled with the zipper of her handbag and pulled out a check. "I almost forgot to pay you. Daddy made out the check this morning."

It was a very modest amount, but Betty hoped she'd been of some help to the girl. She wasn't as confident about the future as Miss Levenger appeared to be, and was fairly certain that if fate decreed a meeting between her and Norman Mailer, she would not emerge unscathed.

Miss Levenger was quickly gone, leaving behind a cloud of tasteful scent. Probably something concocted by Calvin Klein. Betty faithfully read the *New York Times* herself, and prided herself on being current with high-profile names from fashion to foreign affairs.

Emmie Ruin, when she was still Emily Edwards, the petted teenaged daughter, had had dreams similar to Miss Levenger's. But Sid and Mary had seen to it that she was carefully herded toward the country-club set around Wethersfield, was introduced to eligible young men. Well, she'd found Bob Ruin, and now she was having to deal with him, with middle age, an ailing parent, and her impossible brother. And there were three children, so she had all the terrors that the teen years provide for parents.

At least Emmie didn't have to harbor Sid Senior and

her mother in her own home, as Junior and Wendy did. What if she had taken the path planned by Miss Levenger? Would her life have been profoundly different? Probably not. Her father would still have become ill, she would still have found a Bob Ruin-like person to marry. Her brother would always be Sid Junior.

Betty decided to take a short nap as the afternoon wound down. She found she tired more easily than in the past, even when she didn't exert herself. That's what it meant to get old, she supposed, even though her doctor pronounced her healthy—but things could happen so suddenly.

If the same thing happened to me as Sid, she thought, who would take me in? Who would be there to care for me?

Tina strolled in and looked at her sourly.

"Not you," Betty said aloud, "that's for sure." Then she realized that Tina was pretty much in the same boat as she. No Betty, no Kitty Yummies in the food bowl for Tina.

Betty retired for her nap feeling profoundly insecure and at the mercy of her years and the body that had served her well for more than six decades—but how much longer?

The exotic orchid seemed to glow in its corner as she headed from the dining room toward the stairs. Was it warm enough? Did it need water or more light? Betty wondered, as she gazed for a moment in admiration at the orchid, another creature at the mercy of a stranger's goodwill.

As she closed her eyes, she wondered briefly why Molly had never mentioned the Tommy Crandell case. Surely that was juicy gossip for a newcomer like Betty, even after years had passed. Perhaps she was sorry Tommy had failed to eliminate old Mr. Takahashi. She drifted off to sleep seeing the frail old man surrounded by his orchids.

CHAPTER 5

SHE WAS dizzy when she got up from her nap, and promptly sat down on the bed until her head steadied.

What was this all about? It was nothing she'd ever experienced before. She wondered if the unseasonably warm weather had affected her. Or was it a symptom of something more serious? Betty shook her head to shake off the last of the dizziness and caught sight of Tina watching her from the bedroom doorway. Feline expressions of concern were out of character for Tina. She was probably just hungry again.

"It's nothing. Nothing. Go away." She bit her tongue. Betty had sworn to herself when Tina had been dumped in her lap that she'd limit apparently meaningful conversation to human beings. Never the cat.

The day was darkening, and it was almost time to take the orchid across the street to Ted. And she was hungry, too. She'd forgotten to eat lunch, which was the likely cause of her dizziness.

Betty changed into a tailored white shirt and a gored brown tweed skirt, slipped on polished brown leather loafers, and descended to the ground floor. She didn't think a trip across the street without protection would damage the orchid, since the predicted cold front hadn't yet reached East Moulton. She settled it into a brown paper shopping bag, the better to reveal it suddenly to Ted's eyes. At the last moment, she retrieved Sid Junior's letter from under the clock and stuffed it into the pocket of her heavy plaid jacket. The cold front could sweep in at any minute.

"Remember *K* for key," Arnie Harris had said six months ago. Funny that she recalled his words only today. Then she decided she would track him down when she went upstate and ask him what he'd meant.

"I hope I'm not late, Ted."

"Right on time, Elizabeth. I expect nothing less from you." Ted turned his wheelchair from the door and rolled across the smooth floor toward the kitchen. His only acknowledgment of the shopping bag Betty carried was an almost imperceptibly raised eyebrow.

"Don't worry," Betty said, "it's not edible."

"Good," he said. "You know the drill. The wine's been open and breathing for a while. A really sensational Burgundy tonight. Pour us a glass. We're having tournedos, sort of Rossini. I acquired a decent pâté de foie gras and a not-so-good truffle. Hope it's not too heavy for a meager eater like you. Sample a shrimp or two while I turn the meat and see to the potatoes. I'll be with you in two minutes."

The aroma of the searing beef doubled Betty's hunger. She plucked a plump pink shrimp from a crystal bowl set in another full of crushed ice, then swiped the shrimp through the creamy dip, which had a strong hint of horseradish and a touch of vermouth.

As always when she joined Ted for dinner, she was

quietly impressed with the skill with which he managed his kitchen activities. The range was low enough for him to reach from his wheelchair, the pots and pans were all reachable on their racks via a system of pulleys, the drawers for utensils were at just the right height. She watched him turn the thick rounds of fillet, lower the heat slightly, and move toward the table, where he picked up the glass of wine Betty had poured for him. He sipped and sighed. "Exquisite, and shamefully expensive. What do you think?"

"I think the dollars are probably wasted on me, that's how good it is."

"Don't denigrate yourself, Elizabeth. You are a wise and discerning woman. All right, what's in the bag? What's the favor? And most important, what's eating away at your heart? I know it's something. You can't hide much from Uncle Ted."

Betty took another sip of her wine, thinking how comfortable she was with this young man at least thirty years her junior. She decided to answer his questions in reverse order. "Sid Edwards Senior, my old boss. The cat. A host gift via Mr. Takahashi."

"Sid's dead or ill, you want me to mind that animal of yours, and you brought me an orchid?"

"Very good." She handed him the bag. "I hope you don't find any of it . . . too much trouble."

He peered into the bag. "It's beautiful. I hope I don't murder it. I've often been tempted to buy one when I've been to the greenhouse, but always hesitated. Tina is no problem. All she cares about is food. What about Sid?"

Betty had already told him about her long years at Edwards & Son, and how angry she had been when

Junior had forced her to retire. Of course, she'd mentioned Sid Senior, but she'd never really explained their working relationship, even though she thought about Sid daily, especially when she was alone in the evenings in her little house. But at this moment, when she finally had to share the news about Sid's illness, she felt almost reluctant, as though saying the words would make it all the more real. "He's had a stroke and he's back in Connecticut. Alive but disabled. And something's not right."

Ted looked at her and frowned. "How not right?"

She told him about Junior's proposal that she clear Senior's files, her sense that Junior was almost praying for his father to die, the dreaded nursing home, Emmie and her far-fetched story about her childhood "stuff" in the files. "I just remembered today something the old bookkeeper Arnie said when I left. 'If things get bad, look under *K. K* is for key.' "

"Nothing seems obviously 'not right' to me," Ted said. "What about this Arnie? You have no idea what he was talking about?"

"Arnie was always kind of a kidder. He probably meant nothing at all."

"What's in these files you're going to be working on?"

"There's plenty of 'stuff,' that's for sure. Sid was a saver—orderly, but the quantity was amazing."

"Anything of value?"

"I shouldn't think so. Correspondence, contracts, tear sheets from magazines, things Sid was interested in. He'd worked up a business plan for the company, but never acted on it as far as I know. I suppose Junior would find it useful if he intends to make changes, and I know he's crazy about money, but Sid never stored piles of dollars away in the files."

"Well, other than knapsack and knickers, 'key' is really the most logical *K* word relating to Edwards and Son, is it not?"

"I suppose it is," Betty said, "given what the company does—makes locks. But . . ."

Ted watched her steadily through the long silence. Finally he said, "Your face is a nearly open book, Elizabeth. What have you remembered?"

"I guess I'm thinking that there are other kinds of keys. It must have been fifteen years ago that Sid had me sign some papers about a safe-deposit box—a signature card and all that. He and I were joint holders of the box, with the keys to open it. It was personal, nothing to do with the company."

"And he gave you a key!"

She shook her head. "Never. I don't think I'd recognize a safe-deposit box key if I tripped over one. Besides, you have to keep paying rent on the box, don't you? Well, I haven't."

"Then Sid must have been paying it himself all along. And obviously, somewhere under the letter *K* in the files, you'll find the key. . . . You've remembered something else."

"Nothing much. Except that Arnie used to pay Sid's and Mary's bills. There was always a separate personal bank account for Sid and Mary, and the bills came to the office. So I suppose he could have been paying for a safe-deposit box, even after Sid left for Arizona."

"That's it, then. What do you suppose is in the box?" Ted sounded like a kid on a treasure hunt. "You're entitled to look, since you gave in a signature card. It's probably stuffed full of cash. You're rich!"

"I certainly am not, Ted Kelso. I don't care what it's stuffed with, if it even exists. It's not mine. Sid took care of me financially when we both retired. I have no money worries. Anyhow, even if I find the key, I don't know what bank it would be in."

"How's this for a scenario: Junior knows about the box, knows what's in it, and wants to get his hands on it—but he hasn't got the key. Even if he did, he couldn't use it. That's why he wants you to clear the files, find the documents showing what bank it's in. If the key is there, too, he'll want you to open the box, and he'll claim the contents."

"But Sid isn't going to live forever. When he dies, whatever is in there becomes part of his estate, and it will go to Junior and Emmie. And Mary, his wife."

"If they send Sid off to a nursing home and declare him incompetent or whatever, someone will be in charge of his affairs and presumably have access to the box. Sid has a key, too."

Betty shook her head violently. "I want no part of it, and if Arnie was paying for the safe-deposit box all along, Junior would know about it. All he had to do was ask Arnie."

"He probably did, and this Arnie sounds smart enough to be evasive. That's why Junior needs you."

"He's at the office every day. He could look in the files himself."

"Maybe he has, without success."

Betty thought about it. "He's certainly not allowing his sister to look through the files."

"But if he has an inkling that you and his father share a safe-deposit box, he's going to assume you'll head straight for the right spot, maybe find the key, and then he'll see what you do. He can't get into the box himself, but you can. Be careful, Elizabeth. He doesn't sound like a savory person."

"This is all nonsense," Betty said. "When do we eat?"

"Immediately. Take your place at the table."

"Can I carry anything?" she asked cautiously. Ted didn't like help with things he could do perfectly well himself, although he never turned down assistance in washing up.

"Everything's under control. But, say, why don't you put the orchid on the table. I'll bet it's a real beauty if you got it from Hiro. . . . Ahh." He sighed appreciatively as Betty placed the orchid in the center of the table.

"Mr. Takahashi chose it personally," Betty said. "Ted, why have you never mentioned him and Miho? They're rather oddities in a town like East Moulton. And what about her husband?"

"Miho and her father do sort of stand out in a town like this, which is why they keep to themselves, but Tommy Crandell wasn't an oddity. Just a local boy who didn't marry properly in the eyes of the town. We were pretty good friends for a time. He'd help me out with my beehives—getting them ready for the winter—and he'd do some of the heavy garden stuff I couldn't manage. Then he got himself in a heap of trouble a couple of years back, and I had to find someone else to do the work."

"What sort of trouble?"

"Attempted murder, although I never believed it. They say he plotted to get rid of Mr. Takahashi. A badly contrived 'accident' in the greenhouse."

"Because Tommy wanted to build a development on the land where Mr. Takahashi has his greenhouse and truck farm, and the old man wouldn't let him?"

Ted looked surprised. "You certainly know how to pick up the town's sordid tales."

"I got my information from an unlikely source. The daughter of Tommy's lawyer in the case."

"People were very disappointed when he was convicted, but he only served a little time. Miho and her father aren't really popular hereabouts. I suppose it's human nature to need someone to be prejudiced against, and since there aren't any Jews or African Americans in town . . ."

"So two Japanese people definitely out of the mainstream got the town's attention?"

"Something like that. They're different. Of course, a lot of people from the older generations remember the war, and there was a lot of resentment, too, when he acquired the land. I can't remember who sold it to him. Molly Perkins would know."

Ted placed a loaded plate in front of Betty and took his own place at the table. "I'll have to ask Miho how to deal with the orchid. I've forgotten what I ever knew. A *phalaenopsis*, isn't it? I've never had the time or patience to grow orchids, and my dream of being a rural Nero Wolfe vanished when I started costing out a greenhouse, the plants, and everything else it takes to grow them in quantity. So I visit Miho now and then, and enjoy the fruits of her work. Tommy never liked the idea of being a gardener, not masculine enough for him, although he did all right with the truck farm and the orchards."

"What's become of Tommy?"

"Last I heard he was living somewhere upstate. I don't think he and Miho were ever divorced."

"So he may still be harboring plots against Mr. Takahashi."

"Hey, Tommy's okay. A tendency to go off the deep end, but as far as I know, he hasn't set foot in East Moulton in years. Now what else do you want from me?"

"Junior wants me to come on Monday," Betty said. "Tina will need minding from Sunday afternoon. I could bring her over just before I leave."

"Of course she can live here," Ted said, "but I have a better idea. Why don't you enlist Penny to stop at your house twice a day to feed her? Cats are happier at home. I'd feed her at your place myself, but crossing Timberhill Road and getting up your path and into your house isn't all that easy for me."

Betty knew he hated to admit there was something he couldn't do.

"That's by far the best solution. I'll ask Penny in the morning. One of the Whiteys could do it." All three of Penny's blond boys were called Whitey. She supposed it saved on lung power just to yell "Whitey" once, stopping (briefly) all three from continuing whatever mischief they were invariably into. "I'd even pay them. They'd like that."

"If Penny can't do it, then haul the kitty over here. She enjoys my shelves." Ted waved at his wall-to-wall bookcases, filled with books, CDs, videotapes, and computer and sound equipment, with occasional spaces for a cat to sit and contemplate the scene. "For dessert, I have some ice cream," Ted said. "I didn't feel like baking. Hope you don't mind."

"I'm stuffed," Betty said. "The tournedos were sensational. Ice cream sounds good."

Of course it was particularly delicious coconut ice cream, homemade by an old lady who lived on the edge of East Moulton and hand-cranked it while she watched afternoon soap operas.

"Years ago, when I was still able, I used to travel to the Caribbean almost annually. I've never forgotten the coconut ice cream," Ted said. He sounded sad for the days when he really could do anything. Nowadays, he managed to travel quite a bit—by car around the region and even abroad—to locations where his disability could be handled. The Caribbean was probably not yet outfitted for the wheelchair-bound. "I never thought I'd find anyone around here who made it."

"Ted," Betty said slowly, "I need your advice. What do you think of the idea of Sid going to a nursing home?"

Ted looked thoughtful. "I spent some time in a rehab center, which was almost a nursing home. I hated it. I was eager to get on with my life, even if it had to be lived in a wheelchair. But if Sid is sick enough so that getting on with things doesn't matter anymore, and if home care isn't working out, it might be better for him. On the other hand, if he makes it clear that he's dead set against it, it would just make him unhappier. It's lonely if nobody visits . . ."

"My impression is that Junior and his wife want him out of their lives. I certainly can't imagine Wendy making an effort for him, so she wouldn't visit him in a home, and Mary is always so busy with her social things, so I don't see her dropping by daily, or even doing much home care now." Betty put down her spoon, the ice

cream unfinished. "I would care for him, if I were allowed to. I'd visit every day if he went to a nursing
home. I'd do anything for him."

"You're that loyal?"

"I love him," Betty said, surprising herself. She'd never
talked this way about Sid to Ted or anyone. "He's the
only man I ever did love."

CHAPTER 6

NOT LONG after, Betty mumbled her thanks and goodnights, then rushed through the dark to her safe little house, away from the surprised, perhaps amused, expression on Ted's face. She had never told anyone, not one soul, about the depth of her attachment to Sid Senior, which had lasted from the day they met until this moment. She expected it would last to her final breath. As she reached her door, she was beginning to think that sending Sid to a nursing home might be the best solution, after all. She'd know after she had a chance to see him, to understand what he wanted and what his situation at Junior's home was like.

But what must Ted be thinking about her? A sorry old maid with pathetic romantic dreams? If only he knew the truth. But he was too much of a gentleman to probe, and certainly too gentlemanly to mock her or make a joke at her expense.

It was a relief to sink onto her bed and turn out the light. The cold front had moved in and the warmth of the day had retreated. She pulled the down-filled comforter up to her chin and felt the predictable bounce as Tina jumped aboard and settled down. She tried to sleep, but her mind was too active: Sid at his son's mercy and at the mercy of his illness. That humiliating moment of confession at Ted's place. And what had he said when she left? He'd thanked her for the orchid and said, "It's an exotic creature here among my humble bare brick walls and electronics. Like a symbol of a great exotic passion one never imagined existed." But he had smiled kindly, as though he understood that she had let something slip unintentionally.

When she finally slept, she dreamed of the old-fashioned offices of Edwards & Son, the banks of fluorescent lights way up near the high ceiling, the dusty windows, the clatter of typewriters, and the chattering girls.

Bennie Mallis, that was the name of the boy who drove Junior's car. Terribly good-looking, and all the girls liked to flirt with him whenever he passed their desks. Sid had never liked Bennie. "Too damned smooth, don't trust him an inch," was his opinion. Of course, there was the time he'd caught Bennie pilfering a few dollars from the petty cash box. And worse, he later caught him carting away tools and material from the factory. He got sent to prison for that escapade.

Then she was dreaming that she was walking along the dark hallway that led from the offices to the factory. She could hear the thump of machinery, the drone of voices, but she was walking in pitch darkness. The noise continued.

It was her clock radio, set to turn on at seven o'clock. She raised herself groggily on an elbow. It was seven, and it was dark, a sort of lowering dark outside her bedroom window that meant the sun wasn't even attempting to show itself behind a heavy cloud cover. She could feel a stream of icy air from the window she'd opened a crack. A real February day.

Tina was gone, probably to sit beside her food bowl until someone attended to her demands. Betty lay back on her pillows. The excellent Burgundy had given her a slight headache. She should know by now that red wine didn't agree with her. She listened to the news. The weatherman predicted snow for tomorrow. Then she had to think for a moment to remember what day it was today. Wednesday. Her day to volunteer at the library. The snow would be over by the time she had to travel north on Sunday to Edwards & Son. To Sid.

No reason to get up just yet. She had nothing to do, no business to attend to, no projects to engage her, except to get to the library at noon, and first to ask Penny about caring for Tina. That could wait until she was sure the three Whiteys were safely off to school. She didn't find small children, particularly small noisy boys, especially engaging. The Saks boys were nice enough, and as long as they weren't playing with matches, harmless. If she timed her visit properly, there would be good, freshly made coffee—Penny ground the beans herself—and cookies just out of the oven, but, she hoped, no complex craft project that she had to assist with, marbling a floor or stenciling a border.

The worst that could happen was that she'd get caught up in creating decorations for Valentine's Day or Presidents' Day. Penny never let a holiday pass without a flourish of decorations—Lincoln's black hat and beard, red-white-and-blue placemats, Cupids and arrows—and holiday-themed food: a heart-shaped cake, a cherry pie. She imagined that if there had been any African-Americans in East Moulton, Penny would have rounded them up for dinner in order to declare them emancipated at the end of a family meal on Lincoln's Birthday.

Betty often wondered how Penny's mild and adoring husband, Greg, was able to endure the cornucopias at Thanksgiving, the goblins and jack-o'-lanterns at Halloween, the evergreen swags, silver bells, and much, much more at Christmas. He probably just went along with it. She knew for a fact that he did a heroic job of putting up yards and yards of colored lights at Christmas—on the house and every tree and bush in the yard. Not for the first time, Betty had to admit that she herself was simply not cut out to appreciate that kind of devoted suburban creativity.

"Elizabeth, you're being unkind," she said aloud. "Penny is the nicest neighbor anyone could have." That brought Tina back onto the bed—looking gravely disappointed in Betty for failing to materialize in the kitchen with a can opener in her hand. "Run along, puss. I'll be down in a few minutes."

When she was a girl and young woman, she always started the day with prayers, but that habit had long since passed. Today, however, perhaps because of her visit to St. Jude's, she spent a few quiet moments, praying for Sid to get well, stay alive, stay safe. She felt better at the end, and proceeded to begin her day, with the plan to visit Penny, make a list of things she needed to take on Sunday, people she ought to see. She intended to track down Arnie Harris. She tried to recall where he lived. East Hartford, she thought. Or Manchester. She'd find him in the phone book, if he weren't dead, and have him explain about the safe-deposit box and what exactly he meant by "*K* is the key."

Downstairs, the computer's dark eye reminded her that maybe she should take Ted's advice and learn how to reach people out there in cyberspace. Send messages around the world and get them back, a silent conversation that would occupy her time.

At ten, she decided it was safe to visit Penny. She walked the field between her house and the Saks's place, hearing the frozen grasses crunch under her feet. She could almost smell the coming snow.

"Come right on in, Betty. You're just in time for coffee!" Penny was a petite woman, wearing her usual blue jeans and man's shirt, but at least she didn't have a paintbrush in her hand or a tape measure around her neck.

"Coffee sounds good," Betty said. "But I warn you, I'm here to beg a favor."

"I saw the Federal Express truck yesterday. Have you been doing some Home Shopping Network buying?"

"No, it was a letter from my old company. They want me back for a few days. Do you think you could arrange to have the Whiteys feed the cat? I leave Sunday and return Wednesday. I'll make sure there's plenty of cat food."

"No problem, you know that. You like milk in your coffee, don't you? I think it's sweet that you got yourself a cat, in spite of everything that happened. It's nice to have company."

Half the people in town spent their time trying to think of ways to give Betty company. She was sure if they knew the ill-tempered Tina they wouldn't think it was so sweet. Penny, however, actually seemed to like Tina. The cat was probably a relief from the boys.

"So you're going back to work? What about your place here?"

"It's short and temporary," Betty said. "I'm not planning on leaving East Moulton. It's just some cleaning up to do, and the current boss doesn't want to do it."

I wonder why not? Betty thought suddenly. She didn't believe the story about her knowing what should be kept and what should be tossed. Nothing should be kept, not if Senior was never coming back. Of course, she did know the files better than anyone except Sid Senior, and there might be a few bits worth saving, and even Junior could recognize a business plan for Edwards & Son. He must have looked. If he thought there was money hidden away somewhere, he wouldn't hesitate to search.

"I also hope to have a chance to visit my old boss, Sid Edwards. He's had a stroke and it sounds as though he's not in good shape."

"Tell me about it," Penny said as she set the plate of warm cookies in front of Betty. "Greg's grandfather had a stroke, and it was just terrible. He couldn't move or talk, and he just lay there like a vegetable. Fortunately, they could afford to have a nurse in most of the time, but it was so sad. And you know, I was sure he knew everything that was going on, and understood everything people said. And then, bang. One day he had another stroke and he was gone. A blessing. Oh, Betty! I didn't mean to upset you."

Betty hastily wiped away the tears at the corners of her eyes. "Sid was such a vital man, interested in everything . . ."

"I remember the doctors saying that all strokes are different. Maybe your Mr. Edwards is much better off than Grandpa. Does he have a family?"

"Yes, children and grandchildren, and his wife." Some family. His children and grandchildren were likely praying for him to go away; Mary was probably carrying on bravely, but she surely hated being tied down and would prefer to be going off at will to her bridge games and teas, garden club meetings and shopping expeditions.

"No more coffee, thanks. I have some chores to do to get ready for my trip."

Penny still pressed some cookies on her, and promised to feed Tina twice a day.

"At least Tina's not like a dog that needs constant company," Betty said. "She couldn't care less if anybody's around as long as her meals appear on time."

"I'll have the boys bring in your mail and newspapers, and make sure the snow doesn't pile up if we get more storms after the one that's predicted. And don't worry too much about your friend. Things are never as bad as they seem. Usually."

"You've made me feel better," Betty said. "The older I get, the more I think about mortality—not just Sid's, but mine, too."

"Why, you're as young and spry as you feel," Penny said. "You'll live to be a hundred, like old Mr. Takahashi."

Betty was surprised. "You know about him?"

"Everybody knows about him, but I happened to get acquainted with Miho. Poor kid. She had a rough time with that husband of hers, and the town hasn't been very friendly, although they used to line up to buy her produce, but that business has fallen off since Tommy scrammed. She's well rid of him."

"Ted mentioned that Miho and Tommy are apparently still married, even though he's gone."

"He's not gone. I saw him at the garage a couple of weeks ago, hanging out with his buddies. He probably still wants that land, even after the trouble he got himself into. The town needs more housing, at least that's what Greg says. And he's heard rumors that development plans are being talked about again." Greg sold insurance and mixed with the town's businesspeople. A new development would offer a new market for his insurance sales.

"You say you're acquainted with Miho. Isn't she worried that Tommy will try something again against Mr. Takahashi?"

"It's not her father she's worried about. He gave the land to Miho. It's herself she should be worried about."

CHAPTER 7

BETTY HAD nothing much to do for four days, except to pick up her dry cleaning, load up on cat food, and inform Ted that Penny would mind the cat. She was restless and as gloomy as the thickening clouds. At noon on Wednesday, she made her way to the library to spend the afternoon shelving books and doing little chores for the librarian.

The weather was so threatening that almost no one appeared at the library, so Betty searched the card catalog for books about strokes. She came up empty—it was, after all, a library patronized largely by readers of fiction—so when her volunteer shift ended, she drove to the mall on the highway.

The big chain bookstore greeted her with piles of the latest books by Mary Higgins Clark. She made her way through the aisles, past the young men leafing through computer books and young matrons scanning the shelves of mysteries, to the shelves of the health section. Betty found a paperback called *Living with Stroke: A Guide for Survivors and Caregivers*. It was a start. If the snow piled up tomorrow, she could curl up with the book and learn what she should know so that she could help Sid if the opportunity arose. She felt good for a moment, only to be blanketed by a stifling feeling of depression and grief.

Sid wasn't dead yet, but her Sid was gone. Someone different had been left in his place, immobile and silent. Betty struggled to find a bright side, and there was only this: She wouldn't take Junior's words for the gravity of Sid's condition. She had to see for herself, and having seen it, then she would be optimistic or depressed. Siddie and Emmie were not to be trusted on Sid's condition since their opinions were based on getting the impediment their father represented out of their lives.

Betty clung to the thought that since he wasn't dead, there could still be time to recapture some joy of the good times of the past, if only she were allowed to see him. She drove away from the mall toward home, trying to keep her fear and sadness at bay, eager to get to the book, to understand what had happened and what was likely to happen.

She stopped at the supermarket and loaded up a cart with cat food. Another item on her list taken care of. Two lamb chops for her and some frozen baby peas. A few more food items to carry her through if the predicted snow made travel difficult.

On the last mile before home, she noticed the first flakes of snow beginning to fall out of the darkness.

It snowed through the night, and according to the evening TV weatherman, twenty-four inches might be expected before it ended sometime the next morning. Tina refused the invitation to go outside and curled up next to the heating vent, content after her bowl of Kitty Buffet Tuna Surprise.

Betty opened the stroke book and read. She read about

rehabilitation, institutional-care facilities, speech and other communication problems, resolving difficulties with eating, moving about, getting in and out of wheelchairs and a car. She developed a new appreciation of Ted's problems and how well he managed them, although he had never told her the reason for his impairment. She read about hygiene, dressing, exercising, and therapy for the stroke survivor. She liked the word "survivor." It made it seem that Sid had taken an active role in saving his own life. That would be like him: he had a real will to live. He was a survivor.

All the same, the barriers to recovery of even a part of his former self seemed insurmountable. He would do his best, but she could not picture Mary having the time or patience to provide the support he must need. And certainly not Junior, Wendy, or Emmie.

Miles away upstate, in a long dark hallway in an old brick factory building, two people hunched against the wall, talking softly. The only light was a bare red bulb above a heavy door, marking a fire exit. It was possible to make out the handsome features of Bennie Mallis, who had spent most of his short and fairly unproductive working life in the factory and its offices, except for those few months when he was a guest of the state for a minor crime involving materials that were not his to take. The other person's face was in the shadows.

"The old man's been pretty good to me," Bennie said. His companion shrugged. "You've always been okay, too. I could handle it, I guess. And if I can't, I know someone who will. We kind of exchange favors, if you know what I mean."

"I don't, but see that it gets done," the other person whispered. "Soon."

Betty fell asleep in her chair with the book in her lap and the TV mumbling away in the corner. At around two o'clock, she woke suddenly, dazed and confused, and managed to totter upstairs to her bed.

I want to see him now, she thought as sleep crept over her again. There's no time to lose.

A few miles away, the snow sifted down on the glass panes of Mr. Takahashi's greenhouse and melted quickly from the heat within. The road past the house was an unmarked ribbon of white. The line of footprints from the road to the greenhouse, made when the snow was still only a few inches deep, had nearly filled in with new snow. The snowplows wouldn't get to that road until morning.

Dawn brought Betty a picture of a smooth expanse of white. The branches of the old blue spruce were laden with several inches of snow, and the low evergreens Tina had crouched under only a day or two before in the false warmth were completely buried. But the sky was a clear, pale blue and the sun was beginning to rise. Betty looked down from her frosted bedroom window and could not tell where the path from the front door to her mailbox lay. The mailbox itself was capped with snow; snow reached halfway up the pole. Her doctor had told her to take it very easy when shoveling. Her earlier concern about being ill and alone guaranteed that she would not strain her heart lifting shovelfuls of heavy snow. Besides, she was fairly certain Penny would marshal the Whiteys and send them around to fetch her mail and perhaps even shovel a bit.

Of course, her car was snowed in behind the house, near where the old garage had been. She'd never replaced it after the fire. With luck, after his business day, Greg Saks would bring his snowblower around and do the driveway, so she could drive the car out. Then she wondered how much business an insurance salesman had on a day like today. Maybe Greg would be here soon, after he'd blown away the snow at his own house. She hadn't lived here long enough to experience a deep snow like this one, but Ted had mentioned that Greg had always stopped by to clear out his path and driveway in the past. For the moment, however, she and Tina had food and warmth, and needed to go nowhere.

She would have driven north today instead of waiting until Sunday, to Wethersfield and Sid, to Manchester and Arnie, except for this snow. Cora Welles would have welcomed her even three days early. She glanced out the window again and saw the town plow proceeding along Timberhill Road, a spray of snow shooting eight feet into the air from the force of the blade.

The broadcaster of the morning television news from New Haven talked excitedly about a record snowfall for this date. She was wondering if Ted needed anything that she could supply from her larder, so she only half heard the news item about a "tragic discovery," but became alert when East Moulton was mentioned. The body of Mr. Hiro Takahashi had been discovered around daybreak by his daughter, Miho Crandell, in the greenhouse where he grew prizewinning orchids. He had been strangled with a piece of wire and his body hidden behind sacks of potting medium. Mrs. Crandell's estranged husband, Thomas Crandell of New Britain, formerly of East Moulton, was being sought for questioning.

Betty felt a wave of sadness, remembering the polite old man and the serious but friendly young woman, neither of whom the town felt warmly about. Well, this was a murder she wouldn't be expected to solve. It was up to the police to track down Tommy Crandell. Even if she wanted to rush to Miho in some ill-thought-out gesture of neighborliness, she couldn't get there. Shoveling her driveway was well beyond her strength. Officer Bob, the resident state trooper, would be relieved of the necessity of coldly turning her away while the major-crimes squad of the Connecticut State Police did their business.

Yet Betty was curious. Tommy Crandell might crave that land and see the elimination of his father-in-law as the way to get it, but surely he was not stupid enough to think that the authorities would have forgotten about his previous attempt on the old man's life. Then she shook her head to acknowledge the rapid decline of plain common sense among the younger generation. But she continued to think.

If Tommy had come to the greenhouse in the night, with the snow falling, surely his car would have left some tracks the police would find. She could imagine Mr. Takahashi venturing out to his greenhouse to be sure his plants were warm enough, to be sure the glass panes of the greenhouse were closed against the snow. If Tommy had driven up, perhaps simply to stake out the house, he would have seen the lights on in the greenhouse and Mr. Takahashi moving about. Then, of course, he would have had to plow his way through the drifts to reach the door. More telltale hints of his presence. It would not have been hard to surprise and overcome the frail old gentleman.

Betty made herself some coffee and filled Tina's bowl, then looked around. Tina was unaccountably absent. Probably curled up somewhere snug and warm, but just the same, she checked the closets and floor-level cabinets. Tina had a way of creeping through open doors only to be shut in when Betty came past and closed them.

She heard the low-pitched *whirr* of a motor and carried her coffee into the living room. She smiled at the sight of Greg Saks pushing his snowblower through the pile of snow left by the snowplow and up her driveway. The three boys, armed with shovels twice their height, were digging away at her mailbox, and one had even started on the walk. She checked to see if she had the makings of hot chocolate for the boys and enough coffee for Greg. It wouldn't be as good as Penny's, but at least she could offer something when they finished clearing her walk and driveway.

"And where have you been, miss?"

Tina strolled in, yawning and stretching, circled her food bowl, sniffed, and turned away.

"Turning picky, are you? Well, that's it for this morning. Take it or leave it."

Tina chose to leave it, and Betty kicked herself mentally for again speaking to the cat as though she were a person, then she hurried upstairs to dress, so she was ready when the Sakses were done.

Twenty minutes later, they were at her door.

"Thank you so much," Betty said. "Come in and have something to warm you up. You must be frozen."

The four of them clumped into the kitchen, splattering melted snow on the rag rug.

"It's not so cold, Miz Trenka," Greg said. "Is it, Whitey?"

"Naw," they chorused. And then she heard a gabble of words: "Snowman . . . fort . . . snowball fight . . . sled."

"We've got to take care of Mr. Kelso's place first," Greg said as he took a mug of coffee. "Then you can go play. Say thanks for the hot chocolate."

"Thank you," the boys said in unison.

"How are the roads, Greg?"

"Not so bad. The plows have been through. I got to town earlier without any problem. You shouldn't have any trouble with driving. You heard about the old Japanese guy getting himself killed?"

"Mr. Takahashi?" Betty said. "Yes, I heard it on the news."

"Penny knows the daughter. The old fellow wasn't exactly popular around town, but Tommy Crandell isn't going to get off with a few months for attempted anything this time."

Betty said, "Don't you think it was foolish—if that's the right word—to do this after what he did before? He must have known the police would think of him first."

"I don't know Tommy well, but he never struck me as a Nobel Prize winner," Greg said. "On the other hand, he wasn't silent about how he felt the old man was in his way. Still, it could have been someone else, bent on robbery or something."

"I find it hard to imagine someone stealing orchids in

the middle of a blizzard," Betty said. "There can't have been anything else in the greenhouse."

"Yeah." Greg nodded in agreement. "It must have been someone out to get him. Personally."

Betty shrugged, but she remembered that Molly held the former admiral personally responsible for her brother's World War II death. But she could definitely not picture Molly Perkins or her husband tramping through the snow to strangle someone after all these years. Impossible, unless there were others in town who felt the same way.

After the Saks men trundled off to dig out Ted Kelso, Betty listened to the news on the radio, but there was no further story on the East Moulton murder. Tina went out into the snow reluctantly and soon returned, this time eager for breakfast. Betty mopped up the melted snow on her kitchen floor and went back to her book on strokes. She was now determined to go upstate tomorrow, after she'd fetched her dry cleaning, or on Saturday at the latest. She had to see Sid soon.

CHAPTER 8

BY FRIDAY morning, Betty was uncharacteristically excited about leaving. She'd fixed on Saturday morning. Cora had no objection to her coming earlier than planned. Penny was perfectly willing to take on Tina's feeding for an extra day. The snow was still piled high at the roadside, but occasional cars traveled Timberhill Road at their usual speed; no driving problems there. Her cleaning wouldn't be ready until the afternoon, but at least she could start packing.

The intrepid paperboy had persuaded his father to make the deliveries in his four-wheel-drive vehicle, and thanks to the Saks boys, Betty was able to get to the mailbox where the newspaper had been left. The paper had a longish report on Mr. Takahashi's murder, and it recapitulated Tommy Crandell's previous brush with the law, but apparently he had not yet been located. Harold Levenger, his former attorney, had made a plea for Tommy to turn himself in. Betty wondered how Miss Levenger was viewing the legal profession now. Certainly it wasn't as dull as she had believed it to be. Betty thought she ought to pass by the greenhouse and offer her condolences to Miho. Few people from town were likely to do so.

Around midday, the phone rang. To Betty's surprise it was Miss Levenger herself, sounding a bit shaky.

"I need to see you, Miss Trenka. I don't know what to do. I mean, like, it's too much—and you're so smart. Could I come now?"

Oh, dear, Betty thought. She's been rejected by a prospective employer, or the interviewer had made unwelcome advances but had held out a terrific job in exchange for her willingness to comply.

How had she managed to arrange a job interview so quickly?

"I have a couple of errands to take care of this afternoon," Betty said, "but if you could come soon . . ."

"I'm only up on the highway at the McDonald's. Ten minutes. Fifteen at most." Miss Levenger hung up quickly.

Barely ten minutes later, the doorbell rang. Miss Levenger must have flown along the exit road from the food-and-fuel stop on the highway. Dangerous under these snowy conditions. Betty was prepared to remind her that if she weren't alive she'd never get that glamorous job in publishing in New York.

But it wasn't Miss Levenger. It was Officer Bob, the resident state policeman, at her door, bundled up in an official parka against the chill that swirled into the living room. His handsome face was ruddy with the cold. He carefully knocked the snow from his highly polished boots.

"My word," Betty said. "Come on in, Bob."

"Morning, Miss Trenka. Sorry to bother you so early."

"No bother. Can I get you some coffee?" Bob shook his head. "Then sit down. What can I do for you?"

"It's kind of semiofficial," Bob said. He pushed the

parka's hood from his head. "You've heard about Mr. Takahashi?"

"What a shame," Betty said. "Such a nice old man." Then she looked at him sharply. "You're here about that?"

"Well, we were looking into people who'd seen him lately, and Miho—Mrs. Crandell—said you'd just been to the greenhouse. The only person who had stopped in for some weeks, according to Miho."

"Except, presumably, the person who killed him."

"Ah, well, yes. We're just checking to be sure about— about everything."

"Yes, I was there. I bought an orchid for Ted Kelso. It was the first time I'd met either Mr. Takahashi or Miho. I stopped on an impulse, since I needed something to bring to Ted, who'd invited me to dinner that evening."

"No one else around, I take it? No cars parked along the road?"

Betty shook her head. "And neither Mr. Takahashi nor Miho seemed nervous or scared."

"Meaning?"

"As one might be if someone had threatened them, or someone they didn't want to see had been hanging around. Isn't Tommy Crandell the likely suspect?"

"You know about him, too?"

"It was mentioned on TV and in the papers," Betty said. "And people in town have mentioned Tommy's previous problems with the old man, including the daughter of Tommy's lawyer." Betty didn't miss Officer Bob's deepened interest in her words. "Well, Kathy would know about it, wouldn't she? What's wrong with that?"

"What's wrong is that Kathy used to have kind of a

crush on Tommy. Hell, she used to visit him when he was in prison. Harold Levenger would have a fit if he knew that. Tommy's coming up on middle age. Even if he didn't have all that baggage he's carrying, he's too old for a kid like her. I'd like to talk to her, too. But her folks said she was visiting friends yesterday and got snowed in."

With a sinking feeling, Betty remembered that Miss Levenger was likely to appear any minute, and faced the dilemma that event posed. Should she tell Officer Bob? Surely, glossy Miss Levenger wasn't party to a murder. Betty casually got up and walked to the front window to scan Timberhill Road.

"How long do you suppose this snow will hang on?" she asked. "I have to go upstate tomorrow, and the snow makes everything so difficult." Bob had pulled the state police car into her driveway. If Miss Levenger had any guilty knowledge, she'd surely see it and drive on. Just then, Betty saw a car slow down in front of her house and suddenly speed off. Miss Levenger, no doubt. Now she had no hesitation about speaking of her to Bob. She sat down again in the chair facing the policeman, who had taken the sofa.

"Actually, Miss Levenger was going to stop by here this afternoon. I—I've been working on her résumé, and we needed to make some changes."

The trooper frowned. "Was—or *is*—stopping by?"

"She was supposed to be here long ago. Maybe the snow . . ."

"Miss Trenka, if she appears, please, for her sake, give me a call. Or let her know she must take her troubles to her father. As a lawyer, he's one of the best, and he'll be able to set her straight. Promise?"

"I promise," Betty said, vaguely disturbed by the moral dilemma she had encountered. It was unwelcome, but she was a believer in law and order. "Would it be appropriate for me to visit Miho? I don't imagine many in town are rushing to succor her at this difficult time."

"She is at home, and seems composed, but she doesn't show a lot of emotion to officialdom. I suppose it couldn't hurt—and maybe she'd say something to you that she was reluctant to say to us."

"Such as?"

"Whether she'd heard from Tommy lately. She said not, but you never know. Frankly, Betty, he's our best bet. If only we could locate him."

"Penny Saks said she'd seen him a couple of weeks ago at one of the garages around town. And Greg Saks reports that there's talk again about the housing development Tommy wanted to get started."

Bob was suddenly interested. "Then I may stop by and chat with Penny," he said. "Where did you say you were going upstate?"

"I didn't, but I've taken on a short assignment at my old company, near Hartford. I leave tomorrow, back by Wednesday. Is that okay?"

Bob grinned. "Sure. Why not? I'm not planning to arrest you."

He pulled up the hood of his parka and strode out into the cold. Betty watched him back the police car out of the driveway and head toward the Saks house. She thought that Penny would be rather thrilled to be asked questions about a town scandal—even if she'd have a difficult time persuading Bob to decorate Valentine's Day cupcakes.

He would probably enjoy her cookies, and certainly her coffee.

The phone rang.

"Miss Trenka, why were the police at your house?"

"They were asking about Mr. Takahashi's murder, Kathy."

"But what do you have to do with that?"

"I was at his greenhouse the other day, buying the orchid you saw here. Just routine questions. Where are you?" If she tells me, Betty thought, I will be obligated to tell Officer Bob, little as I like the idea.

"I'm—I'm on my way to somewhere else," Kathy Levenger said.

"You really should go home and talk to your father. About Tommy, I mean. He's in a lot of trouble."

"I know." Miss Levenger almost wailed. "I don't know what to do."

"Helping a fugitive isn't going to be good for your career," Betty said. "You know what's the right thing to do, and doing the right thing is always best."

Kathy Levenger didn't deny that she was helping a fugitive Tommy Crandell. "I just don't know what the right thing is under the circumstances. He says he didn't do it."

"And you believe him." Betty sighed inwardly. "Listen, Kathy. If you don't want to be party to turning him in, send him on his way and protect yourself. Remember, if he did kill Mr. Takahashi, he probably wouldn't hesitate to hurt you. And besides," Betty added, almost irrelevantly under the circumstances, "he is a married man."

"Oh, that." She dismissed Miho. "Well, you're smarter

than I am, so maybe I'll just leave him here and go home."

"Where is here?"

"This place near the highway. The kind of bar place."

Betty knew it. A sort of roadhouse near the entrance ramp to the highway. "Get away right now." She used the firm voice she'd always used with recalcitrant office workers—the girl who persisted in playing loud rock music while she input data, the receptionist who chewed gum while answering the phone. Even Bennie Mallis once when he'd slouched in and plunked down in the reception area and put his feet on the round glass coffee table.

"Yes, Miss Trenka." The voice had apparently worked with Kathy Levenger. "But I really . . ." She stopped. Betty imagined Kathy had been about to confess her undying passion for the increasingly unsavory Tommy Crandell. Now Betty was eager to get her off the phone, so she could call the Saks house and inform Officer Bob of Tommy's whereabouts.

"I understand, dear. But it's the right thing to do. Trust me." She thought she heard a gulping sob as Kathy Levenger hung up. She dialed Penny quickly.

"Penny, is Bob still there? It's very important."

Betty explained to Bob what Kathy had told her.

"All right! Got to run," he said brusquely. Then he added, "Thanks, Betty. You're an okay gal."

"I hope Kathy doesn't get hurt," Betty said.

"Me, too."

She hated being an informer but it was the right thing to do.

A few minutes later, Penny called her back. "What did

you say to Officer Bob? He was out of here like the devil was after him."

"It was something about Tommy," Betty said reluctantly.

"He's not going to get off with a few months this time," Penny said. She sounded almost gleeful. "Wait till I tell Greg. So you're leaving tomorrow, right?"

"Right. Got to pick up my dry cleaning now, and maybe visit Miho."

"I should do that. Tomorrow," Penny said. "I've got cupcakes in the oven, or I'd go with you. Give her my love. No, better say sympathies. It sounds more polite. Love might seem too familiar. But ask her if I can bring her anything. I've got bread in the freezer, a nice tuna casserole, anything she needs."

"I'll do that," Betty said, and wondered whether tuna-noodle casserole was what an alien being, left alone by murder in a small Connecticut town, really craved.

CHAPTER 9

BETTY PROCEEDED with care along the road to East Moulton center. She liked the feel of the substantial Buick, and felt secure in her driving, if not in her mind. First of all, she felt guilty about involving Miss Levenger in the hunt for Tommy. She wouldn't think Betty was so damned clever now. Molly Perkins would already have heard all the latest gossip, and she even had an excuse to stop at the pharmacy. As she intended to visit Miho, she decided that she ought to bring some little gift to brighten Miho's day of sadness. At a craft show she'd bought a couple of lovely handmade candles decorated with perfect little dried rosebuds. One of them would do for Miho. She needed some tissue paper and ribbon to wrap it, and happily, Molly had a small section in the pharmacy devoted to wrapping papers and greeting cards.

Of course, Sid wasn't ever far from her consciousness, although her decision to drive to Hartford a day early had eased some of her anxiety. How she would manage to persuade Mary that she should see him hadn't been considered. She supposed she could fall back on the nursing home situation: she needed to find out his wishes before she discussed it with the family.

It was easiest for her to park in the well-cleared space in front of the dry cleaner's, pick up her clothes and leave them in the car, and then walk back up the cleared sidewalk to the pharmacy, where there were no shoveled parking spots. Perk wouldn't dream of shoveling snow. When she was a girl, the boys used to be eager to earn a few dollars shoveling snow on days like yesterday when school was canceled. Maybe it was beneath kids nowadays, or maybe Perk considered it a waste of money to pay for moving snow that would melt eventually.

"Well, look who's out and about. A regular snowbunny, aren't you?" Molly bustled, as always. "How's the driving? I didn't find it bad. Not like last winter. Well, you weren't here for that, but it was some storm that hit us in January." Betty went to the rack of gift wrap because Molly clearly didn't expect a direct response. "Isn't that lovely paper? Imported. Don't sell much of it, but it's nice to have if someone's looking for something special." Molly leaned forward eagerly, to hear why Betty would want special wrapping paper.

"What?" Betty realized she had to say something. "I was planning to visit . . ." Miho, with the father Molly hated so much. How would Molly respond? Then Betty decided she wasn't going to allow small-town prejudices to hamper her style. ". . . visit Miho. Offer my condolences. I had a little something to bring her, and thought I'd wrap it nicely."

"Wasn't that the most terrible thing?" Molly actually looked a bit stricken, but not for long. The need to gossip coursed through her veins. "If you're not safe in your own house . . . And then after what I said to you the other day, I was afraid the cops would be questioning me about the old man. But it was Tommy, had to be—even though he's denied it. That Levenger girl is saying he was with her the whole time. Swears to it. I don't know what these girls are coming to, saying they were with some guy all night. Of course, her father was his lawyer on the other case, so maybe they got something going. He's too old for her, anyhow. You must have seen her around . . ."

"I know Kathy Levenger," Betty said. She picked out some ribbon with a golden sheen that matched the tissue paper she'd selected. "So they caught up with Tommy at the roadhouse, then?"

"You know about that? I heard about it myself only a couple of minutes ago."

"I told them where to go," Betty said. "I didn't think it was a good idea for Kathy to be on the run from the police, especially since murder is so serious."

"How did you know where they were?"

"Kathy called me for advice. I told her to go home to her father—his advice would be better than mine any day. And I couldn't not tell Officer Bob about the whereabouts of a man he suspected of murder, now could I?"

"I suppose not," Molly said. "Well, in the end, they let him go. I suppose they had to believe the girl, although you'd think grown men trained in police work would have better sense than to believe a wild young thing like Kathy Levenger. You can bet that Harold Levenger told him to get out of town and stay out, so he's probably gone home. They're saying he lives in New Britain or someplace like that."

"I'll just borrow these scissors for a minute to cut some ribbon," Betty said. She wasn't eager to speculate on the wildness of Kathy or the whereabouts of Tommy.

She paid for the ribbon and paper and went to the door. "I'll be leaving tomorrow. I hope there's no more murderous excitement while I'm gone."

"This town," Molly said, with a shake of her head. "I don't know what it's coming to."

In the car, Betty wrapped the candle in tissue paper and tied each end with the ribbon. Her gift looked quite presentable. She drove through town to the road leading to the greenhouse. She was still cautious, but the blacktop was clear of snow. I'm *too* cautious, she thought. I should be bolder. She pictured herself marching up to the big white Edwards house off the Silas Deane Highway in Wethersfield and demanding to see Sid. How boldly would she react if Mary or Wendy or Sid, Emmie or one of the grandchildren, told her to go away?

The snow in the parking area in front of the greenhouse hadn't been plowed, but it had been flattened, probably by police and other vehicles that had swarmed in on the news of Mr. Takahashi's murder. There was a single dark car parked near the greenhouse door. The path to the front door of the house was untouched, however, but Betty could see a shoveled path from the back to the greenhouse. The lights appeared to be on, although she didn't see anyone moving about.

She tried the greenhouse door, and it opened, as it had the other time she'd been here. She stepped inside quickly, so the cold air wouldn't damage the orchids, which surrounded her with exotic shapes and a fantasy of color. It was fairly warm here and dampish, so she loosened her scarf and removed her knit cap.

"Ah, Betty-san." Miho looked tired and drawn, but she forced a gentle smile and patted her dark glossy hair.

"I came—I mean . . . I'm terribly sorry about your father. He was so kind to allow me to buy the orchid." She held out her little gift to Miho, who took it and ducked her head in a kind of bow. "Penny Saks will come around to see you. She sends her sympathies." And probably a box of homemade muffins.

"Penny is my good friend," Miho said. "I am grateful for your kindness and hers."

"Could I ask you what happened?"

"No, you could not." Betty hadn't noticed the tall, muscular man who had followed Miho into this part of the greenhouse, as he had remained hidden by a large fernlike plant that appeared to be thriving in the warm, damp space. "I'm sick of you town gossips prying into our private business."

Miho folded her hands as if in an effort to calm herself. "This is my husband," she said.

Betty looked up sharply. Tommy Crandell was an ordinary-looking young man—not really so young, either, with a slightly receding hairline, in his forties perhaps. He had to be that, at least, if he had served in Vietnam, as Molly claimed. He wore a white T-shirt that showed powerful arms, with a tattoo on his right biceps. He looked grim, but maybe he was merely being protective of Miho.

"I'm not here to pick up gossip," Betty said. "I met Miho and her late father a day or two ago, and was so sorry to hear of his death. My name is Elizabeth Trenka . . ."

Tommy Crandell lowered his head and glared. "You're the bitch who told the cops about me!"

Betty wouldn't again quickly trust Officer Bob to

protect his informants. "I was worried about Kathy, and wanted to keep her from trouble."

"She's got no trouble," Tommy said. "We were out late the other night, and she let me stay in the rec room in their basement for the night. I was there the whole time. Her father knew it. Miho will tell you I didn't have anything to do with offing the old man."

"Is that so, Miho?"

"I have told the police that I looked out in the night and saw that the lights were on in the greenhouse. It was snowing still, and I was worried that my father had gone there without a coat, so I came here. There was someone here who was not my father—a man—but it was not Tommy. He pushed me down and ran into the night. I hear a car, and then I look for my father. He is dead." She gestured toward the floor beneath a shelf holding pots filled with tiny yellow orchids. "I tried to help him—I have medical training—but I could do nothing, so I called the police. They say they will find Tommy, but it was not Tommy who killed my father." She squeezed her eyes shut as if holding back tears. "It was another man." Tommy moved up behind her and wrapped an arm around her. Miho seemed willing to sink into the security of his arms.

"I see," Betty said. "I'm sorry I intruded." Suddenly Sid slipped back into her mind. As defenseless as old Mr. Takahashi, who at least died surrounded by his fabulous orchids. "I wonder, Miho. Would it be possible to purchase another orchid? The one I got for Ted was so beautiful, and I have a sick friend who might enjoy . . ."

Miho selected another *phalaenopsis* and handed it to Betty. "Take it. No charge. You are a good friend." She raised the wrapped candle as though to prove Betty's friendship. "Take paper to wrap it against the cold." She seemed unwilling to detach herself from Tommy's arms.

Betty fumbled and managed to wrap a length of white paper around the orchid. "My old boss had a stroke, and I wanted to get him something lovely to look at. I'm driving up to Wethersfield tomorrow to see him, so I can bring this along." She looked up from wrapping the plant to see that Tommy had retreated into the depths of the greenhouse. "Will you be all right, Miho? You're sure Tommy had nothing to do with—with anything?"

"It was not Tommy I saw here," Miho said. "He would not harm my father, even if they said he tried to before. I think my father made up the story because he did not like Tommy, who wanted to tear down the greenhouse and build houses on the land." She half smiled. "Maybe he will build houses now, but he cannot have the greenhouse. I will care for the orchids, as my father would have wished."

Betty went home to pack and think about the puzzles of Miho and Tommy, Kathy and Tommy, and the mysteries of the way men die.

CHAPTER 10

ON SATURDAY morning, Betty set out for Wethersfield and Sid, uncertain how she would be received—if anyone was willing to receive her at all. For a time, she sat in her car and debated with herself over the route. She could go south and take the Connecticut Turnpike over the Connecticut River, then head north, directly to Wethersfield, or she could take the route on this side of the river toward Manchester and East Hartford, cross the river at Hartford (even stop to check in with Cora and Dave), and drive the few miles south to Wethersfield. In the latter case, she might even detour to Manchester and check a phone book for Arnie Harris—the one call to the information operator indicated that there were a couple of A. Harrises. Initially she had decided to see if Arnie still worked at Edwards & Son, for Sid Junior, before trying to locate him, but the temptation to see him at once was—well, it was like the temptation to see Sid immediately, and not wait for the family to grant her an audience. With Mr. Takahashi's murder, she hadn't dwelt much on her own coming job at Edwards & Son, but as she drove along the turnpike toward Old Saybrook, she felt apprehensive. She didn't want Siddie hanging about—looking over her shoulder while she emptied the files—or Emmie, either. She didn't want anyone there if she found the alleged hidden safe-deposit box key.

The mighty bridge spanning the Connecticut River gave her a view of marinas at Essex, crowded with yachts and cruisers in storage for the winter. Off to her left, she could see the railroad bridge that carried Amtrak trains between Boston and New York. It was still a drawbridge that opened to allow tall ships passage in and out of the river. And to her left, on the banks of the river, sat the town of Old Saybrook, and the exclusive Fenwick beach resort area.

At the end of the bridge, she took the highway to the right into Essex itself and then on upstate, past Deep River and the road to Gillette Castle, a pale brown stone fort perched on the edge of the water. The road was lined with forests belonging to one of the state parks, and finally there was Haddam, which harbored Wallace Stevens's "thin men," and a number of ways of looking at a blackbird. Middletown, Cromwell, the road to Berlin and New Britain, the abode of Tommy Crandell, Rocky Hill, and then Wethersfield.

She was getting cold feet. And it wasn't just that the snow along the roadside seemed deeper here. The caution that was so much a part of her character was nudging her toward skipping Sid and proceeding to Cora and Dave Welles, to consider her plans at leisure. Maybe Sunday would be a better time for a sudden visit. Sid might have therapists or nurses about today, and she didn't want to share him with them. Or she could run over to Grafton, near East Hartford. Someone might be at the Edwards & Son offices, someone who could tell her something about Arnie. Then there were the files. She knew how the personnel records had been kept in her day, and that wasn't so long ago. She swerved and caught herself as her mind wandered to her key chain. The key! Of course. It wasn't the key Arnie had been talking about, but she still had the key to the heavy door of Edwards & Son. She'd always had it because she often worked late, even later than Sid, who was expected home for dinner at a reasonable hour. Mary had the reputation of being a superb cook, even though they had a housekeeper.

Many's the time she encountered the night watchman as she was locking up. Bennie Mallis had that job for a time, until Sid had him arrested when it was discovered that he spent his night-watchman hours loading material from the factory onto a truck at the loading dock. She could find the files easily, since she couldn't imagine Sid Junior taking it into his head to reorganize the personnel files. He was not very fussy about details or organization. She didn't imagine he'd bothered to change the locks, either, although that would have been simple enough. That's what the company manufactured.

She began to get excited. If she got into Edwards & Son today, she could look around, before Siddie and the others were there. She might find what they expected her to find, and then she'd have time to figure out what she should do about it. It was only early afternoon. There was plenty of time. She'd stop and pick up a sandwich, and if she encountered anyone at the office, she'd make up a story.

That's not so cautious, my girl, she thought. That's bold. She drove through Wethersfield, catching sight of some familiar places, but continued to the turnoff to the bridge that would bring her to East Hartford, and only a couple of miles beyond to the depressed little manufacturing town where Edwards & Son was located—on a dingy street lined with warehouses, abandoned factories, and a few bars and lunch places that catered to the factory workers. Everything was familiar to her now as she neared Edwards & Son.

They'd never bothered to fill in the huge pothole just before the stop sign at Maple Street. Probably never was a maple tree there since the Revolutionary War. Maple Street itself was constructed out of cobblestones, and while she never wore high heels because of her height, the office girls used to complain constantly about the rigors of walking across the street in their stiletto heels.

Snow was piled high along the curb in front of the dirty redbrick building with a few Victorian flourishes. It looked grim and stark against the pale sky. She stopped the car and looked up at the four stories. No lights, and even on a sunny day, the place was dark enough inside to warrant having the lights constantly on.

Betty checked around the front door for signs of an alarm system. Part of Sid's plan for a new direction for the company had been to develop electronic alarms and locking systems for older buildings like this one, but Junior apparently hadn't pushed in that direction—at least not to the point where such a system existed and served as a showcase installation for the firm. She saw no evidence of any kind of alarm.

Click. The substantial key turned in the classic Edwards & Son lock. She twisted the old-fashioned brass knob. At least Junior was continuing to maintain the old tradition of keeping the brass fittings highly polished. A rush of warm air greeted her, tinged with dust and echoes of cigar smoke and perfume. Junior continued to smoke fat, expensive cigars, making him unexpectedly trendy, and the young women of the office staff continued to believe in the efficacy of scent in their daily lives. Three steps up, through a glass door, and into the reception area, she could see the shape of the receptionist's desk, very large, grand, and curved. Daylight filtered in through the fan light over the main door, but it was otherwise almost impenetrably dim.

She felt the wall to the right of the glass door. Two switches, one for the light over the desk, one for the banks of lights for the whole reception area. Then she hesitated. The watchman would be alerted if he saw lights, but she quickly relaxed. If the remembered pattern was still in place, the watchman checked the doors only in late afternoon on weekends, as people in the past had often worked on Saturdays. But apparently not today.

The place was silent and seemed to be empty. Lights didn't matter. She knew the way to the offices with her eyes shut, so she shut her eyes and walked—and almost tripped on a new area rug near the cluster of chairs for visitors and the coffee table on which Bennie Mallis liked to rest his work boots. Wendy had probably been in a redecorating mode and had decided that a too-divine rug on the black-and-white tile floor would be just the thing.

Betty stretched out her right hand to guide her along the hall. Junior's office first. The door was shut. She listened but heard nothing. Then she checked the floor to see if a sliver of light showed from beneath any of the doors. Sid's office, with its row of filing cabinets, was across the hall from Junior's, but she was saving that for later. She wondered who, if anyone, now occupied her office next to Sid's. She continued along the hall: the men's room; the ladies' room; and opposite them the wide alcove that served as the copier area. A tiny green light glowed in the dimness and startled her. The fax machine.

Finally she reached the big doorless room where several cubicles housed the accounts payable, accounts receivable, and order-fulfillment departments. Arnie had had his bookkeeping desk here in the corner, with his own bank of two-drawer metal filing cabinets. The woman who dealt with human resources and personnel issues had a cramped little office just beyond the big room, and farther along the hallway were offices for salespersons, a conference room, and the door to the factory.

She almost felt like crying. It was all so familiar and nostalgically comforting, but it was no longer her world. Betty continued along to the personnel office, a room with no windows to show light. She closed the door and switched on the overhead lights. Nothing seemed to have changed in the six months she'd been gone. The blank face of a computer stared at her. Human resources, indeed—as though all those hardworking human beings were like fossil-fuel resources, hidden oil wells to be pumped dry. She didn't know who ran the department now, but whoever it was had the sense to lock the files. Commendable, but few had the common sense to keep the key on his or her person. If the key got lost, locksmith hell would ensue, although certainly the factory foreman used to know how to unlock anything.

She slid open the top drawer of the personnel person's desk. There it was, among the paper clips and Post-it notes, a flat silver key on a tagged ring. She inserted it into the cylinder on the corner of the three-drawer cabinet and opened the drawer labeled *A–L*. She found the hanging folder for "Harris, A.," and took it out. In a moment she had Arnie's address in Manchester, his phone number, his employment history. He appeared to be still alive, but working only part-time, starting shortly after she'd left Edwards & Son. Junior was probably easing him out, but for once, in a kindly way. Arnie's wife, Sophie, she recalled, had a chronic illness, so even a little income to supplement Social Security and keep up health insurance was probably welcome.

At least she knew where to find Arnie. What now? The deep silence of the building was beginning to unnerve her. Funny, she used to like being here when the building was unoccupied and the phones silent, with no one to disturb her concentration.

Then a phone began to ring, out at the receptionist's desk. The personnel desk had a busy lamp field attached to the phone, so one could tell which extension was ringing and which ones were in use, but the phone itself didn't ring in this office. She could see that the number ringing was the main number. Then the faint ringing stopped, and she saw that the call had been picked up by Extension 105. Junior's extension. Quickly she turned out the lights in the personnel office. She didn't want to be discovered by Junior, or whoever it was who had answered. She opened the door a crack and listened, but there was nothing to hear. She hadn't seen another car parked in front of the building, but Junior would have put his BMW in the factory parking lot rather than leave it on the street. There had been no sign of light in Junior's office, but, of course, he had windows, so perhaps lights weren't necessary.

As she peered down the hall toward Junior's office, she heard a door open. She shrank back. Then she looked again, peering through her thick glasses at the two people who emerged. The tall man was vaguely familiar, the other unrecognizable as either a man or a woman, bundled up in a heavy coat with a knit cap pulled down over the ears. They headed through the reception area to the main door, and in a few seconds, had departed. Betty breathed heavily, her heart pounding.

She was beginning to regret her determination to be bolder, but at least they were gone for the moment. Who was the man she'd seen? It looked very much like Bennie Mallis, and the other could have been Junior, or possibly Emmie's husband, Bob Ruin. Neither of the latter was particularly robust, but Bennie's swagger was practically his trademark. So Junior had brought him back after his father was gone. She didn't like that one bit, and felt her annoyance rising.

Then she remembered that it wasn't her company to worry about any longer—and wondered if Sid knew that Bennie was back in touch, in some fashion, with the firm. But alas, even if Sid knew, had perhaps overheard something Junior said, he couldn't express his thoughts. He could only lie there in silent rage, unable to form words that Junior could understand.

She waited in the personnel office for several minutes, in case the men returned, but the building remained dead silent.

There was time, she thought, to slip into Sid's old office and look under *K* in his file. She felt a little reckless as she opened the door to his office and turned on the light, but caution guided her hand and her movement toward the admittedly ugly filing cabinets. The labels on the drawers were still as she remembered them. No *A* through *C*, though. There, in Sid's familiar printing were words: FUTURE PROJECTS. SUPPLIERS. PERSONAL.

She pulled open the drawer labeled PERSONAL, thinking it was the best place to start. Here the hanging folders were divided alphabetically, and she found a file marked K. It was empty except for a 10×13 manila envelope, sealed with shipping tape. It wasn't very fat, as though there were only a few sheets of paper in it. She folded it over and crammed it into her pocket.

It was time for her to get out, go to Cora and Dave's, and plan what she would do tomorrow.

Betty crept softly down the hallway to the front door and looked out cautiously. Her car was where she had left it. There was no traffic on Maple Street, no other parked cars, and even the luncheonette across the street was closed. She took a deep breath and ventured out. The heavy door clicked shut, locking itself behind her. She went quickly to her car and started it.

The orchid for Sid, snugly wrapped in white paper, rested on the seat beside her. She hoped it was surviving the cold, although it was far warmer today than yesterday.

It was only when she glanced in the rearview mirror that she saw the man standing close to the building, half hidden by a pile of snow, leaning forward as though watching her.

Panicked, she didn't make a U-turn, but drove straight

down Maple Street to the service road that would take her behind the luncheonette and then back to the main road. That way, she didn't have to pass directly in front of the waiting man.

This time she knew who it was. Bennie Mallis had been posted to watch the unknown car parked in front of Edwards & Son. Bennie Mallis, or someone very like him.

CHAPTER 11

BETTY FOUND that she was clutching the steering wheel with unusual force. Her shoulders were hunched and tense, and in her stomach, she felt a little knot of . . . what? Fear? Too strong a word. It was more like anxiety and confusion. Of course, Junior had a perfect right to keep track of the people who let themselves into his company offices, but still, the fact that Bennie was there on the lookout unsettled her.

A glance in the rearview mirror did not reveal a pursuing car. Then again, why would he follow her? Bennie must have recognized her, and since he knew who had been in the building—and surely knew or would know from Junior that she would be on the scene on Monday morning—tracking her now was pointless. Still, feeling a bit foolish, she took a circuitous route out of East Hartford—to the bridge over the Connecticut River to Hartford. There wasn't much traffic on this snow-covered Saturday afternoon, and even if Bennie had decided to trail her, he wouldn't have had much difficulty, even on the side streets she took. She crossed the river and found herself in downtown Hartford, with the golden dome of the State Capitol Building on the horizon. Then she reached the outskirts of the city, which gradually eased into the more affluent suburbs, toward West Hartford.

Cora and Dave Welles, and once upon a time, Betty herself, lived in a so-called garden apartment complex, a gathering of two-story units with tiny yards in back. (For the garden, although she'd never bothered to plant anything, except for a couple of terra-cotta pots of geraniums and petunias.) The units looked out on a square common, which in the warm weather boasted a green lawn and a few decorative shade trees and forsythia and mountain laurel bushes. Each unit had a little front porch for relaxing on lazy summer afternoons.

The parking lot behind the complex had been well plowed, with each space assigned to residents to keep space-hungry parkers from using it. A big fine if you parked without a permit, but Cora had assured her that she had a visitor's permit for as long as she stayed with them. Space 51 was to be hers for the duration. It was a less desirable space because it was near the rack of trash barrels and a longer distance to the complex. She pulled into the spot, then patted her pocket to be sure the envelope from the *K* file was still there. For a minute she was tempted to rip off the tape and see what it contained, but something held her back. She got her suitcase from the backseat and tucked the orchid in her other arm. She hoped Cora wouldn't fall upon it with cries of thanks, but Cora wasn't a plant person, so she had a hostess gift for her in her suitcase. Cora was definitely a Godiva chocolate person.

She couldn't help but glance at the unit that had been hers. A child's sled was propped upright in the snow near the front porch. Surely her little one-bedroom place was too small for a family with children. In any case, children were discouraged, since most of the residents were seniors. On the other hand, the complex was highly desirable, being well-managed, close to schools and shopping. Or maybe someone had grandchildren here for a visit.

Dave flung open the door before she had a chance to ring the bell. "Betty! Betty, come on in. We were getting worried about you." Dave Welles was broad and bald, and consistently jovial. He grabbed her suitcase and gave her a hug, calling over his shoulder, "She made it, Cora! Say, you're looking just great, kiddo. Retirement agrees with you." She followed him into the living room, just as Cora rushed from the kitchen, drying her hands on her apron.

"We expected you earlier," Cora said. "Didn't have car trouble, did you? With all this snow, you never know." Cora was about Betty's age, but small and thin with fluffy reddish hair and bright curious eyes. She looked almost dithery, although Betty knew from experience that she was a formidable cardplayer who could bluff with the best of them.

"Now you just sit down and I'll get you some coffee. Dave, you put her bag in the guest room and come right back. Don't go planning renovations in there and forget about us." Dave did as he was commanded. Cora eyed the wrapped orchid. "I hope you didn't go and get me a plant," she said. "Killed an African violet only last week."

"No, this is for Sid," Betty said. "A sort of special thing I thought might cheer him up. I know what you like."

Cora almost clapped her hands. "I should have known you wouldn't forget my chocolate habit. How is Sid doing? And tell me what took you so long to get here. You couldn't have forgotten the way. Here, let me take your coat."

"No! I mean, let me get something from the pocket." She pulled out the envelope and held on to it tightly. "I was late because I had a stop to make," Betty said. She wasn't sure whether she should confess the details of her detour to Edwards & Son right away. Cora was, if anything, more cautious than Betty, and would surely disapprove. But Betty didn't have a chance to tell her anything—she was out in the kitchen pouring coffee. She decided to wait for Dave and tell them both at once. Dave was a pretty sensible guy, and would probably look at the issue of the lurking Bennie in a comfortably straightforward way. But she wasn't going to look at the envelope until she was alone.

"I wanted to talk to you about Sid," she said when Cora was back with the steaming coffee mugs. "I don't know anything more than I told you—the stroke and being incapacitated and all. But I'm afraid Junior and the family will make difficulties about me seeing him. But I feel I must see him right away. So I was thinking . . . maybe I should just drive over to Wethersfield tomorrow and present myself."

"And be turned away on the doorstep?" Cora shook her head. "Think of something better. So they'll have to let you in."

"I suppose I should call first," Betty said.

"Ha! Then they could turn you away simply by hanging up. Isn't there some important business you have to discuss with him?"

Betty shook her head. "All business was finished when I left. Mary Edwards would never believe that; neither would Junior. Besides, from what I gather, Sid isn't in any position to discuss anything, even if he does understand what people are saying."

"We'll ask Dave what to do. He's a great improviser. Why, the way he can fix anything that's broken with just a little piece of wire— Dave! Where are you?" Cora turned to Betty. "He's been fretting about the windows in the guest room. Every time he gets near them, he's got to check the drafts and test the locks. Dave!"

"I'm coming, hon." After a moment, Dave appeared. "I was just checking the heating vent. Don't want to freeze Betty to death now that we've finally got her here. Up for a few hands of poker or gin tonight, kiddo?"

"I'm out of practice," Betty said, "but I do miss our games. It would be like the old days." Sitting here with her friends, she realized how much she did miss the daily visits, the regular card games, the conversation with people her own age who faced the same fears about old age and illness. "I sometimes wonder why I ever moved away."

"You said yourself, sitting right there on the sofa in this very room, that you wanted a clean break from those old days you miss so much. With Sid gone, you said you didn't have anything to keep you here." Of course, Betty had confided a lot of her feelings about Sid and their history together to Cora, who was certainly not a gossip, but a good listener. "If you ask me, he should have gotten rid of that wife of his and married you years ago."

"That's an old story," Betty said, "not worth retelling."

"Corabelle, don't stir up memories best forgotten,"

Dave said. "Not with the old boy lying sick." Dave stretched out his arms. "At least I've got my health. Today, anyhow. How's yours, Betty?"

"A few aches and pains from time to time," she said. "I'm doing fine. My doctor says I have the constitution of someone years younger."

"That's something," Dave said, and started to fidget. "Look, I've got a woodworking project . . ." The units shared a large common basement where Dave had set up his shop. "I'll just run along and see you girls later."

"Wait," Cora said. "Betty needs some advice."

Betty explained about wanting to see Sid tomorrow, despite the apparent reluctance of the family to allow her to do so.

Dave thought for a minute. "They churchgoing people?"

"Yes, as I recall. Mary was always pretty active in her church's affairs."

"Then if you feel you've got to do this, why not hang around on the street until you see her leave? Then you pop in, and whoever is there, a nurse or somebody, won't try to stop you."

"Yeah, it could very well be Junior who answers the door." It looked pretty hopeless, and she didn't think she was up to lurking on the street waiting for Mary Edwards to leave for church. Her foray into Edwards & Son earlier had pretty much proved she wasn't cut out for undercover stuff. "I don't think I could do that, Dave—not that it's not a clever idea."

Dave stroked his chin and looked serious. "You're right. Creeping around isn't your style. You're more up-front, straight on."

Betty shrugged. "Not so straight on." She told them about her visit to Edwards & Son, although she said nothing about *K* is for key or the envelope she'd found in Sid's files. "At least I got the telephone number of Arnie Harris, the old guy who was the bookkeeper when I was there. He should have an idea of what's what. He and Sid were pretty close, so he's probably been keeping up with his health situation."

"I understand how much you want to see Sid," Cora said. "I know what I'd be going through if it was Dave, but he's right. Once you're back in the office, you'll figure out the lay of the land; then you can twist Junior around your little finger, and there's no way he's going to keep you from seeing Sid. Why don't you call your friend Arnie and see what he has to say?"

So she called when Dave had taken himself off to his workshop. Sophie Harris sounded wary until Betty identified herself.

"Why, Miz Trenka! Not a week's gone by since you left that Arnie hasn't mentioned you. The old place could sure use you now. We've been wondering what had become of you."

"I didn't have your address, or I would have sent a holiday card," Betty said. "Is Arnie okay?"

"He shouldn't be? The man's as strong as a horse."

"Still at Edwards and Son?"

Mrs. Harris hesitated. "Things have changed. He's kind of part-time now. Funny thing, though. Mr. Edwards Junior called just a few minutes before you did, and Arnie was off to the factory to meet him. I don't know what it was about . . ."

"Tell Arnie I'll call him when I'm back at the office on

Monday, or maybe tomorrow if I have the chance. I'm going to be doing some work at Edwards and Son for a few days."

She was eager to hang up. If Junior was at the Edwards & Son offices with Arnie, then he couldn't be home with his father, barring her way to Sid. First, though, she had to look at what was in the envelope.

The guest bedroom wasn't the least bit drafty. She got Cora's box of chocolates from her bag, sat down on the bed, and pulled the tape off the envelope.

There were a couple of sheets of paper inside, and another small white envelope with the name of a bank in the corner: Connecticut United Bank. That didn't tell her much. Conn United had branches in practically every town in the state. The small envelope held something hard. When she opened it, a flat, odd-looking key dropped into her hand. She didn't doubt for a second that it was the much-discussed safe-deposit box key. Was it hers or Sid's? One document in the big envelope was a contract for the safe-deposit box, the one she and Sid had signed years before, and named the branch of Conn United Bank in Grafton, only a short distance from Edwards & Son. It was the branch where the company had its accounts, and that was where the box belonging to herself and Sid was. Now she really did need to speak to Arnie, to find out exactly what the deal was. She looked at the second sheet of paper. It was a note, badly typed, on Edwards & Son stationery. It must have been typed by Sid, since he was not much more than a hunt-and-peck typist. It said:

Betty dear. In the box this key fits is property of mine that belongs to you and you alone if anything should happen to me. What you'll find are things I've acquired for you, things I would have liked to have given to you before but could not. This is a private matter between the two of us, and you don't need to mention it to Mary or the children. They are well taken care of, but you, who have given me so much, deserve much more in return.

He had signed it, "Love, Sid."

She sat and looked at the letter for a long time, until she remembered that she had to get going.

"I'm going to Wethersfield, after all," Betty told Cora when she emerged from the guest room, the key safely stowed in the dresser drawer. She could handle Mary, and even Emmie if she happened to be there, although it was difficult to imagine Junior welcoming both his sister and Bob Ruin into his overcrowded home. But Emmie might be paying a visit to her ailing father, although Betty's recollection of her did not include memories of selfless devotion to her parents. Still, Emmie said she often stopped by to read to him, so if she wanted Betty's help with extracting her "stuff" from the files, she might be willing to help Betty in return by easing her way to Sid.

"I won't be gone long," Betty said, and Cora nodded. "I don't like driving at night, anyhow, and it still gets dark pretty early."

"I'll heat up a nice chicken potpie for supper," Cora said, "unless you'd like to go out to eat."

"Dave would probably rather stay home and get out the cards," Betty said. "Staying in is fine with me."

She picked up the orchid, and the memory of poor

dead Mr. Takahashi rose and retreated. She stopped at the door and turned back to Cora. "If anything delays me, I'll call you."

By the time Betty reached Wethersfield, the light was dimming, although it was by no means late. She hoped that Junior and Arnie had a lot of business to discuss that would keep him there for a good long time.

The street in front of the Edwardses's distinguished colonial house was clear of snow, as though the town had taken pains to remove the snowbanks piled up by the plows in this pricey neighborhood. The house stood on the top of a hill with an expanse of snow-covered lawn sweeping down to the street. It was dotted with leafless trees, including an elegant cluster of white-barked birches. The driveway was all uphill, and it seemed to be covered with a sheet of ice. Betty wasn't sure her car could handle it, so she chose to park on the street—probably forbidden by the town, but she'd risk a ticket—and walk up the nicely shoveled brick walk to the front door.

She knew her hands were trembling as she reached out to ring the doorbell.

CHAPTER 12

SHE COULD hear the bell chime inside the house, that deep, refined, ruling-class *dong* she used to envy as a child when she visited the homes of WASP-y friends. It was so different from the shrill, tinny *ding-dong* of the bell at her parents' house. Not that their bell was often pushed. Ma's friends came and went without knocking or ringing, Pa didn't have all that many visitors, and, really, only the mailman with a special delivery or a package rang, or people collecting for charity.

Betty waited for the door to be opened, feeling more nervous as the seconds passed. She imagined someone had peered out from behind the snowy, gauzy white curtains that covered the front windows, seen who it was, and was deciding how to turn her away.

"Betty! What a surprise!" Emmie Edwards Ruin had colored her hair a honey blond, and it fell in a youthful pageboy to her shoulders, held in place by a black velvet band on the top of her head. "Come in!" All of Emmie looked youthful. Her figure was as trim as Betty remembered, but perhaps the tight eyes and smooth neck were the result of careful, expensive cosmetic surgery. She

106

wore a loose lavender silk shirt and a tailored fawn skirt, with tiny pearl earrings and a string of ladylike pearls at that enviable throat.

Betty entered the foyer, feeling comparatively awkward and lumpish in her heavy tweed coat and sensible shoes. Of course, the orchid in its wrapping and the handbag over one arm made shaking hands with Emmie difficult. "You're looking very well, Emmie," Betty said.

Emmie brushed back a hair from her forehead. "It's not easy, under the circumstances. Dad's illness, the company . . ."

"I was hoping," Betty said carefully, "that I might have a few minutes with your father. If he's able, I mean. I wouldn't want to . . . If your mother would allow . . ."

"Mother has sort of retreated into her own world since they've been back. Just getting him here took so much out of her, and there's so much that has to be done to care for him. And then there's the usual confusion with Wendy's kids trying to lead normal teenage lives, while sharing their home with the grandparents. Bob and I aren't staying here, thank goodness. We're at a hotel outside of Hartford, and it's costing us a fortune. I go home to Westport every few days to be sure the kids haven't turned the place into a crack house or something. Actually, all three of them are away at college, speaking of costing a fortune. I try to come by every day when I'm here to see Dad. I like reading to him, since he understands absolutely everything, and I help him with some of his therapy. We have therapists and the like who come in, but he seems to enjoy having me around. At least he has a woman who's here almost 'round the clock to look after him. Siddie condescends to discuss business with him occasionally, but that only upsets Father."

"Are there problems with Edwards and Son? You mentioned . . ."

"Siddie is going off on tangents, as usual," Emmie said wearily. "You know what he's like. He's going to run the place into the ground, and then what will be left for me? Dad's condition costs plenty, too, although he's well-enough fixed. As you would know." For the first time, Betty caught a hint of the old resentment about Sid's attempt to assure her financial well-being in retirement. What would she say if she knew about the safe-deposit box with its unknown contents?

Betty would have liked to know more about Junior's "tangents," but there was time enough for that on Monday. Today, as long as she'd made it this far, she wanted to see Sid.

"About your father . . ."

"He's probably sleeping—that's what he mostly does—but since you've come all this way, maybe Mrs. Potter has him sitting up . . ." Emmie walked a short distance into the foyer and Betty followed. Emmie suddenly looked back over her shoulder. "Don't expect much, Betty. Don't expect anything at all. He's not the man you knew; he's not my father. He's just a thing, there on the bed." Her voice caught, and Betty was moved by Emmie's unexpected show of emotion. "He may not even know you, although it's hard to tell what he recognizes."

She led the way to the broad staircase with a beautifully carved newel post of polished mahogany. The carpet was a lovely pinkish peach and the wall was papered with a delicate stripe in pale green, with just an occasional line of the same pink as the carpet. A series of innocuous, tasteful watercolor landscapes in thin gilt frames marched up the wall to the top of the stairs.

On the landing on the second floor was a row of closed doors, all glossy white with no offending fingerprints.

"Mother is resting in her room," Emmie said softly, and tilted her chin toward a door at the head of the stairs. "Father's room is down here to the right. It used to be the master bedroom, but, of course, Mother had to move to her own room. We put him in the biggest room because he needs so much stuff, and because there's a little dressing room attached that we fixed up for Mrs. Potter, so she can have some privacy and can sleep over. We're lucky, you know, that he can afford things others might not be able to. We went through hell finding someone to look after him. Mother just can't do it, and I certainly can't. If he starts being able to move around, we'll probably have to fix something up downstairs, since he won't be able to manage the stairs for a long time, if ever. The therapist seems to think he'll soon be ready for a wheelchair. I don't know how he'll take to that."

Betty thought that Ted Kelso probably had the answers Emmie needed, but she was determined not to offer advice or opinions. She felt like an intruder as it was.

"Siddie said he mentioned to you the need to convince Mother to put Father into a nursing home," Emmie said. "That would solve a lot of problems."

"He might not want that," Betty said cautiously.

"He has no vote in the matter, really," Emmie said. Her voice was tinged with temper.

"I think," Betty said, "that if one tries to carry out the wishes of a dead person, one certainly should try to do the same with someone still alive. He is your father. Yes, I think he does have a vote in a matter like this."

"A lot of help you're going to be," Emmie said crossly as they reached the last closed door on the landing. Betty was aware that the smell of sickness was stronger: sour, sweet, and faintly nauseating. "Mother isn't thinking clearly. It's almost as if he's already dead and she's wrapped up in grieving for him. She doesn't seem to realize that it would be best for him—and her—to get him out of the house. He can't go on this way. . . . We can't."

She turned the knob and pushed open the door.

The room was dim, with curtains drawn, and the smell of age, medications, and bodily discharges was almost overpowering. Betty glanced at the bed, a high hospital bed with protective sides to keep a person from rolling out, but it was empty, a jumble of sheets and pillows.

"That damned woman has him sitting up!" Emmie said angrily.

Betty followed her into the darkened room and saw a gaunt, hunched figure in a chair by the window, although the curtains prevented anyone from seeing out. "Mrs. Potter! Come in here!"

The head of the person in the chair seemed to move at the sound of Emmie's voice. It had to be Sid, but Betty was almost afraid to approach him, to see what he'd become.

"Should he just be sitting here in the dark?" she asked.

"I mean, it's a lovely sunny day out. Maybe he'd like to have something to look at."

"He wouldn't notice," Emmie said. "Mrs. Potter! Now!"

Again, Betty saw the head move. He was certainly noticing Emmie's voice.

Suddenly a door opened in the long wall of the room; a sturdy gray-haired woman emerged, yawning. "I was having a little lie-down, Mrs. Ruin." This was presumably Mrs. Potter. "It wears a body out moving the old fellow around."

"What's he doing sitting up?" Emmie said.

"He seemed to want to," Mrs. Potter said. "No harm in that. The therapist says it's good for him to be out of bed, to keep him from getting those nasty pressure sores from lying in one place all day. I can't keep rolling him from one side to the other all day. And he's getting stronger on his right side, you know—and he's quite good at helping to transfer himself to the chair."

"Thank you, Doctor," Emmie said, but Mrs. Potter didn't seem to notice the sarcasm. "This is Miss Trenka, an old friend of Father's." Betty saw his head move at the sound of her name. "Betty, this is Mrs. Potter, Father's aide." She moved around the bed to her father's chair.

"Pleasure," said Mrs. Potter, without displaying any. Then she said to Betty in a low voice, "Don't go thinking he doesn't understand what you're saying, because he does. He just can't answer. He can make maybe a few sounds, and sometimes they come out like real words. But he wasn't struck stupid, no matter what the son tells you."

"Does he like to sit in the dark?" Betty asked. She felt distinctly uncomfortable at this first meeting with Sid.

"Well, what's the difference? He can't read, really; he can't concentrate on the TV for more than a few minutes. And it's an effort to get from the bed to the chair, so he kinda dozes once he's sitting up."

Betty saw Emmie gesturing for her to join them.

"Dad, here's Betty Trenka to see you. You remember Betty, don't you?" Emmie was speaking loudly, although Betty didn't remember that Sid had been hard of hearing.

Finally Betty was face-to-face with Sid Edwards. She struggled not to show by her expression how changed he looked—so old and frail—with his once-handsome features somehow blurred and softened by his illness. She noticed that his left hand gripped the arm of the chair, but his right dangled loosely.

"Hello, Sid. I'm so glad to see you."

Their eyes met, and Betty saw his pleasure in recognizing her. He did recognize her, and he tried to speak. She was sure she heard, "Hi," or maybe it was just a heavy sigh, but there was something on his face that could be a smile. "Hi." She heard it again, and this time she was sure. She felt like weeping, whether from joy at his recognizing her, or her sorrow at the lost person she had known.

"There, you see?" Mrs. Potter had trailed after them. "The old fellow does talk a bit, doesn't he? Are you comfortable, Mr. Edwards? Need a pillow?"

Betty saw only that his eyes flickered in Mrs. Potter's direction, but she seemed to understand him. "He's okay for now. I've got so I can read him pretty good."

"I have some rather important things to do," Emmie said. She was growing impatient. "I'll be back later, Dad, to read to you. You and Betty have a nice visit." Then she said to Betty, "Don't spend too much time with him. He tires easily. Just come downstairs and give me a shout when you're leaving, and I'll see if Mother is up to seeing you." Then she was gone.

Mrs. Potter moved a straight chair over to a spot near Sid. "Have a seat. No point in standing up. Mr. Edwards hears perfectly well, so you don't have to shout like that one does. I'll be in my room if you need anything."

At last she was alone with Sid.

"I would have come sooner, Sid, but I only just heard from Siddie about your illness."

There was that slight twitch to his mouth that she knew was a smile.

"I know you can understand me, and you know that I'll be able to understand you."

He reached out his left hand, which seemed to function well enough, and took her hand. His skin felt thin and papery as he squeezed her hand. His eyes never left her face.

"Everyone says you're improving." She looked down at the white paper bundle she was still carrying. "Look, do you really want to sit in the dark? Squeeze my hand twice for no and once for yes."

He squeezed her hand twice. She set the orchid down on the table next to the bed and pulled back the curtains. The pale light of an approaching winter's evening filled the room.

"That's better," she said. "We had a lot of snow yesterday, so it's a winter wonderland out there. And look at this." She took the paper from around the orchid. "I couldn't resist it, it's so beautiful. It was grown by a man who was murdered just the other day, an old Japanese man who lived in my town. I'll tell you about it another time." Sid nodded, or seemed to. Then he looked at her anxiously.

"Oh, it's rather nice living in East Moulton. Friendly people, lovely neighbors, and my house is as cozy as can be." Sid seemed satisfied with her answer to a question unasked. How did she know what he wanted to know? Because he'd asked the question with his mind, the way he used to, and she'd understood. "And you'll be surprised to know that I have a cat."

Sid's brow wrinkled briefly.

"You're right. I don't like cats—but I didn't get it on purpose. It just came to me, dumped in my lap by a friend from years ago." She waited a minute, then said, "I suppose you're wondering how Siddie came to be in touch with me." One squeeze. She would have to be careful about explaining her coming task, if knowing his office was being cleared out would upset him.

"I'm here for another reason, Sid. I mean, I wanted to see you, but Junior thought it wouldn't be wise." She was surprised at the strength of his grip. It was neither yes nor no; it was annoyance. "He said that you and he had agreed that if your office at Edwards and Son needed to be cleared out, I was the one who was to do it." The grip relaxed. One squeeze for yes. "I know you hate to think that you can't come back." He signaled yes. "But Junior seems to have plans . . ." She held his eyes and tried to read what he was thinking. He seemed downcast, and perhaps far away, reliving the old days when he was in charge.

"Do you want me to clean out the files?" Yes.

"Is there something in the files you don't want Junior to know about?" Yes.

"I think I've already found it. It's the key, isn't it? A quick yes. "I was at Edwards and Son this morning, and I looked in the files. I read your note a little while ago. Will you try to tell me what's in the box?" A firm no.

"Should I ask Arnie Harris about it?" Another quick yes.

"I tried to reach him today, but he had gone to the office to meet Junior. I'll try him again tomorrow. Don't worry, Sid. I'll take care of everything." This time, it was an emphatic yes. Betty smiled, and sat there holding his hand for a few minutes. She noticed then that he seemed to have fallen asleep. The strain of a visitor had worn him out. She placed his hand carefully on the arm of the chair and stood up. As she started to walk toward Mrs. Potter's door to tell her she was leaving, she heard a sound behind her and turned. Sid's eyes were open . . . and he was watching her.

"Hi," he said. "Hi."

"I'll be back, Sid," she said. "Every day if you want . . . but maybe not tomorrow. We still have a lot to talk about."

Sid's left hand made a fist. Once. Yes. Then he seemed to be trying to form words.

Betty leaned toward him. "What is it, Sid? Don't look so worried. Try again."

It was as soft as a summer breeze, but she heard it distinctly. "Careful," he was saying.

"You want me to be careful? Is that it?" She could tell by his eyes that she'd heard it correctly. "I will. I know there are things going on. Junior has brought Bennie Mallis back to the company, but I'll see what can be done about that."

Sid frowned for a minute, then relaxed, and she was sure there was a faint smile on his face. Approving, because she'd understood. Then he became agitated, as though trying to stand. Perhaps the mention of Bennie had upset him more than he'd let on.

Betty brushed away her tears as she knocked on Mrs. Potter's door. "I'll be leaving now," she said.

Mrs. Potter emerged. "There, there, now, Mr. Edwards. Don't excite yourself." She straightened the sheets and pillows on the bed. "It's getting near time for the evening news. We'll get you settled in bed for that." She turned to Betty. "He likes watching the early news, likes to keep up with what's going on in the world. Amazing, isn't it? Then I bring up his supper. Mrs. Edwards used to bring him his supper and help him eat, but she's kinda given up on that, although she still cooks for him and the family. Emmie comes around often, and sometimes the young Mr. Edwards, although Mrs. Edwards Junior hasn't ever set foot in this room as far as I know. Never mind, he's well looked after—even if his wife can't face seeing him, and having the responsibility for him."

"I'd do it," Betty said. "I'd do anything for him, except . . ."

Mrs. Potter was moving Sid from his chair to the bed with surprising ease. "Except it's not your place. I understand."

While Mrs. Potter was off in the corner turning on the

television set and closing the curtains on the falling dusk, Betty said to Sid, "I promise to be careful. Of everyone. Good night, my love."

The orchid was a bright spot in the corner of the dim room. She left quickly before he tried another heart-wrenching "Hi."

CHAPTER 13

THE HALLWAY outside Sid's room was quiet. The whole house was quiet—and then she heard women's voices from downstairs. Shrill and angry, and she felt a knot of alarm in the pit of her stomach. She was sure Mary was complaining about her presence.

She slipped down the stairs and out the front door without being seen, then kept her mind blank as she drove away.

It was dark by the time she got back to Cora and Dave's. From the parking lot, she could see them moving about in the kitchen. When she let herself quietly into the living room, the smell of chicken potpie filled the place, and Cora was singing in the kitchen. The table in the dining alcove was nicely set—Cora had used the good china she was so proud of. She'd bought it in England a couple of years before, right after Dave retired and they started traveling.

Betty didn't want to talk to anyone just yet, not even Cora and Dave. She crept silently into her bedroom, shut the door, and lay down on the embroidered spread. She thought about Sid with mixed emotions.

Sid could say a few words; they could still communicate in the old way. He'd told her that Junior shouldn't know about the key she found in the files. He'd warned her to be careful and told her to talk to Arnie. The worst part of his situation, other than his disabilities, was that he was under the care of someone other than his wife, who wasn't willing to do much caretaking in any case.

She fell asleep, thinking she really ought to tell Cora she was back, so she wouldn't worry.

A knock on the door woke her.

"We were beginning to get frantic," Cora said. "You said you'd call if you were going to be late."

"I—I just couldn't talk to anyone," Betty said. "I'm so sorry. It was thoughtless of me."

"I ended up having Dave call Mrs. Edwards to see if you were still there."

"And what did she say?"

"It must have been the son who answered," Dave said. "Very abrupt he was. Something about you interfering where you weren't wanted. Whatever did you do?"

"I saw Sid. It was—it was so sad. But he knew me, and we understood each other. I'll go back, no matter what Junior says."

"Dinner's ready," Cora said, "and Dave's champing at the bit—for the card game. Think you can manage it?"

Betty swung her feet onto the floor. "I'd better manage," she said. "I can't spend the rest of my life living in the past. I wonder how that miserable cat of mine is getting along without me."

The cat was far from miserable. Tina had just recently feasted on top-of-the-line cat food contributed by Penny Saks as a special treat, and dished out by the oldest

Whitey, who expected to be rewarded for his efforts when Miss Trenka returned home. Whitey had taken this opportunity to enjoy half an hour in front of Betty's television set—a luxury for him to be able to choose what he wanted to watch, instead of being supervised by his mother and involved in arguments with his brothers. The lights were on, of course, and Tina had strolled in to cozy up to him, but Whitey was startled when the doorbell rang. What to do? Miss Trenka hadn't told his mother that someone would come calling, and he assumed that grown-ups always informed people when they were going to be away. He thought about ignoring whomever it was, but the bell rang again and again.

Whitey sighed. One of the cable channels was showing *Goosebumps*, and he didn't want to miss the impending horror the show had been building up to. Maybe there was something even more thrilling waiting on the doorstep.

He went to the door.

"Oh, hi." Kathy Levenger certainly didn't alarm Whitey, although as a fashion statement, she was somewhat remote from his mother. A multicolored velvet hat that reminded him of Dr. Seuss hats, a fluffy red coat, and gold-heeled boots. "Is Betty here?"

It took a minute for him to process that Betty was Miss Trenka. "Nope."

"Darn! I need to see her. Do you know when she's coming back?"

"Dunno. Next week, I think. I'm just feeding her cat."

"You wouldn't know where to find her?"

Whitey shook his head. "My mom might know. She's next door."

"I guess it doesn't matter. I got a job interview on Monday, and I needed her advice—like how much money to ask for and stuff."

"My dad says I can get a paper route next year. 'Course, Miss Trenka's going to pay me for feeding Tina."

Kathy Levenger wasn't really listening. "A friend of mine fixed up the interview with some guy who knows a guy, who knows . . ."

"Contacts," Whitey said, with assurance. "My dad says contacts make the world go round."

Kathy laughed. "And I heard it was love. You shouldn't be standing here with the door open. It'll use up all of Betty's heat. Besides, Tommy's waiting for me in the car, and he gets impatient."

Whitey glanced over his shoulder. The show was over, and he never got to see what was hiding in the closet. "I got to go home myself, or my mom will be over here to get me."

"Well, if Betty calls or comes home, ask her to call me, would you?"

"Sure," Whitey said, already having forgotten what she said.

Kathy Levenger crunched along the walk that the Whiteys had shoveled, and could be seen getting into a black car. Whitey thought it was an Acura. Nice car, but he'd better not hang around here much longer or he would really catch it at home. He checked the water bowl and the bowl of dry cat food. Tina was all set until tomorrow. Whitey went home.

Kathy tossed the ridiculous hat into the backseat. Tommy could be so rude about clothes he didn't like.

"I'm dropping you home now," he said. "The cops still think I did the old man, even though Miho says it wasn't me. But I better stick close to New Britain, so they know where I am and don't think I'm trying to run."

"I know you didn't hurt Mr. Takahashi," Kathy said. "You're too nice."

"So you say," Tommy said. He stared out the window for a moment before turning the ignition. "But there're things I've done—might do—that aren't quite . . ."

"Quite what?" She loved it when he got all serious and mysterious. It was like real life or something.

"Nothing. Life is no picnic. You should hear the stories the guys you meet in prison tell you."

"But you'll drive me to my interview, won't you?"

"Meet me in the parking lot of the supermarket on Monday around nine. I don't want your father seeing me driving away with you."

"Daddy was your lawyer. And I have a perfect right to spend time with anyone I want."

"Whatever you say. I got to get an early start on Monday, 'cause I have some business upstate myself."

Betty didn't call home, or call the Sakses, so Whitey didn't have to remember to tell her anything about Kathy Levenger. Instead, Betty was sitting at Cora and Dave's dining-room table, being dealt some good hands. She was a little ahead of Dave in their gin game, although Dave didn't seem to mind. It was just the two of them playing, because Cora insisted on doing the dinner dishes herself. Betty would have preferred to be out there in the kitchen with her, going over her impressions of Sid, her worries about him being there without much loving care. Oh, she supposed Mrs. Potter was okay. She seemed competent and all, but it wasn't the same as having someone who really cared looking after you.

"Gin!" Dave said triumphantly. "Got you now, Betty. Cora, are you going to be out there all night? Whose deal, Betty?"

"My mind is mush, Dave," Betty said. "I'm going to call it quits for tonight. We can play again tomorrow."

Dave was disappointed, but he shrugged it off. "Okay, it's a date. I've got my book to read. This guy, Harlan Coben, writes about a sports agent. Mysteries. Good stuff."

Betty joined Cora in the kitchen. She was peering out the window over the sink, looking at the parking lot, dark except for the lamps at each corner.

"Somebody's out there," she said. "Standing behind one of the cars near the trash barrels. He's been there for half an hour or more. I don't like it. I'm having Dave call security."

Betty remembered the lurking figure of Bennie Mallis at Edwards & Son. Maybe he had trailed her to the apartment complex. But she hadn't seen anyone following her. And why would he be lurking around spying on her? Certainly nobody knew she was here, for one thing. Except maybe . . .

"Cora, when Dave called Sid Edwards's house about me, he didn't say where I was staying, did he?"

"I don't think so," Cora said. "Oh, maybe he said he was the friend you were staying with, but . . ." She turned to face Betty with wide eyes. "You don't think that person out there is checking on you? Why, Dave only spoke to the Edwards son. The young Sid, isn't it? He wouldn't come out on a Saturday night to hang around in our parking lot."

"No, no. Of course not," Betty said hastily. "I'm just all nerves after seeing Sid today. The poor man. I don't know that he's getting the care he deserves. Mary doesn't seem to take any interest. . . . She certainly didn't bother to look in while I was there. And the lady who does care for him says Mary doesn't even bother to bring him his meals. She lets the caretaker do it."

"I told you what I think," Cora said. "It's been a blow to her, and she hasn't put the pieces together yet. Want another cup of coffee before we turn in? Or a nice cup of tea? I remember caffeine doesn't bother you at night. Well, it bothers me. I'm going to have a glass of ginger ale. Dave! You want anything before I go to bed? And come on out here. There's a man hanging around the parking lot."

Once Dave got involved in the problem of the watching man, things happened. He called the security office, which promised to send someone to check on the man. Pretty soon, long blades of light from two flashlights cut through the night. They approached the cars lined up in the parking lot, and in a minute they were at the back door.

"Nobody there, Mrs. Welles," the security man said. "Say, it's Miss Trenka, isn't it?"

"Hello, Mr. Morgan. I'm just back for a visit."

"We figure some kid was sneaking a beer out of sight of his betters. We found an empty can, footprints. You keep your doors locked, Cora, and we'll be checking back later."

The security men trudged away into the night. "We've

had a couple of break-ins over the last few months since you left," Cora said. "They caught one kid, some genius who decided to go into the music business, starting with somebody's CD player. Otherwise, we don't have any trouble."

"It's such a safe place," Betty said. "My little house seems very exposed, now that I think of it. I guess no place is really safe anymore."

"I keep the iron and the ironing board in the hall closet if you want to do any pressing," Cora said. "We'll be up pretty early, since Dave likes to get to early mass."

"I think I'll come with you," Betty said, surprising even herself.

Cora frowned. "As long as I've known you, Betty Trenka, you never went to church with us."

"People change," she said. "I guess I'm worried about Sid."

"Or your immortal soul," Cora said, sounding very much like Sister Mary Joseph, the supervising nun of Betty's childhood school days.

"Well, the church can be a comfort," Cora said. "But if you change your mind about going, I won't say a word. I hope you brought boots; it's supposed to warm up tomorrow, and the streets will be flooded when all this snow starts melting."

"I'm prepared for anything," Betty said. And she felt she was, now that she'd at least had a chance to see Sid, and to know they could communicate. She promised him again in her heart that she'd be careful.

CHAPTER 14

IN A tastefully decorated dining room, in a distinguished white colonial house on a hill in Wethersfield, Sid Edwards Junior, his wife, Wendy, his sister, Emmie, and her husband, Bob Ruin, sat down to a late Saturday night dinner presided over by Mary Edwards, looking worn and tired but regal.

Mary was dressed in a gray dress that exactly matched her coiffed hair. A brooch in the shape of a spray of lilies of the valley, set in diamonds and emeralds, was the only flashy touch. Sid had enjoyed giving her nice jewelry.

"How dare that woman come here to my home," Mary said in an even voice. Junior and Wendy exchanged a look, intercepted by Emmie. It was, in effect, their home now.

"Mother, she did Father a lot of good for years and years, and even today. I haven't seen him so alert and . . . well, happy since he got back here," Emmie said.

"And I suppose it was her doing?" Mary said. A slight frown creased her noble brow.

"He doesn't have that many visitors," Junior said. "It must have been nice for him to see an old friend. She's going to be working for us for a few days, so she'll probably

126

drop in again. Betty's okay, and she's going to be doing us a big favor."

Mary's mouth was set in a hard line. "I can't imagine what that would be."

"Don't be surprised if she talks to you about getting Dad into a nursing home."

"He won't go."

"Then she's going to persuade him to go."

"Am I to have nothing to say about what becomes of my husband?" Mary rearranged the napkin on her lap and speared a green bean with her fork. Then she sighed. "I suppose it would be a relief to have him someplace where I knew he was being looked after properly. I simply can't do it, and I have no life to speak of hanging about here while Mrs. Potter runs things to her own liking."

"It would be a relief if he were out of this situation," Emmie said. "He's never going to get better, however many thousands of dollars we spend on therapy and I don't know what else."

"On Mrs. Potter," Junior said. "For openers."

"I don't know, I think it would be cruel to put him away in a home." Bob Ruin's comment was not taken well. "Of course, if he were to die, problem solved. Apologies for mentioning it, Mother Edwards."

"You certainly have a way of cutting to the heart of the matter, Bob," Mary Edwards said. "But I can face the facts. He's likely to have another stroke at any time and be gone in an instant."

"Don't talk that way," Junior said. "It would create all kinds of problems if he died before I have things settled."

"Things?" Emmie said sharply. "What the hell are you up to, Siddie?"

"Nothing, Sis. I want to get some information together is all, and Betty Trenka's going to help."

"She's going to help me, too," Emmie said. "She said she would."

"I don't know about all of you," Bob Ruin said, "but I've got problems of my own."

Mary Edwards rewarded her son-in-law with a look that said eloquently, What else is new?

"Sid isn't going to die," Mary said. "Someday, of course—but he's got a strong will to live, and he's improving every day. I know he likes having Emmie read to him, even if he's able to read himself. It's just that the paralysis in his right hand makes it hard for him to hold books and turn the pages. I can't bear to see him struggle to do things he did so easily before."

There was a long, uncomfortable moment around the dinner table as Mary held her head up bravely in the face of her tragedy.

"Excellent dinner, Mother Edwards," Bob Ruin said. "You're one hell of a cook. If you'll all excuse me now, I have to meet a guy about some business. I won't be late, Em. I'll pick you up before midnight and we'll be back at the hotel in half an hour. But be sure to leave the door unlocked, in case you doze off in front of the TV. I've lost my key."

"Oh, Bob. How many times have I told you . . . ?" Mary was not pleased.

"I'm sorry. It's probably in a pocket somewhere. We'll lock up when Em and I leave for the hotel."

"What sort of 'guy' do you have to meet at this hour?" Emmie said sourly. "Does your bookie need to be paid off tonight? I don't want to hang around here until you get back. Can't you drop me off now? I want to do my nails and a lot of other stuff."

"Em," Bob said warningly, "I want you to wait here. It would take me out of my way and make me late. I said it's about business. The guy's leaving for the West Coast tomorrow, so it has to be tonight."

Bob sauntered off to his meeting, leaving a silent table behind him.

"What kind of business is he involved in now?" Junior asked finally and rhetorically. "Oh, well—as long as it doesn't cost the family any money."

"Now just a minute, Siddie. The family money is partly mine, you know." Emmie glared at him. "And if I can help Bob . . ."

"Children," Mary Edwards said, "let's be clear about one thing. The family money belongs to your father and me, as long as we are alive. You two will have to wait for the inevitable. The company is your father's and mine, too, no matter what tricks Siddie pulled to get rid of him."

"Mother, let's not start on that again," Junior said. "He'd outlived his usefulness to the firm, and if I hadn't gotten him out, he would probably have handed over everything to Betty Trenka. She got enough out of him as it was."

Wendy Edwards stood up suddenly. "I'm going to clear the table now. I can't stand hearing you bicker about poor Sid and Betty, who's a perfectly nice woman who was loyal to Sid and the company for practically forever. Why, she'd been there for years already when we got married, Siddie. Remember? And I got her that nice clock when she retired. She was there when the kids were born."

"Where are those kids anyhow?" Sid asked. "They'd better not try staying out till all hours again tonight."

"They're not comfortable here," Wendy said. "They're always thinking about their grandfather sick upstairs, and being quiet so they won't disturb him, and never being allowed to have their friends over. I'm sorry to say it, Mother Edwards, but it's terribly hard on them, just as it's hard on all of us. I do think he'd be better off in a nursing home." Wendy piled up the dirty dinner plates and took them to the kitchen.

"Mrs. Potter's gone home," Mary said. "She said Sid would be all right tonight without her. So I guess you'll have to get your father settled down for the night, Siddie."

"I hate heaving him around, and he doesn't like me touching him, either. I thought Mrs. Potter was always on duty. Don't we pay her enough for her to do her job properly?" Junior was angry.

"You know she doesn't stay on Saturdays," his mother said. "And she's only a home caretaker, not a trained nurse. They say it's good for someone in Sid's condition to have family members attending him. I'd help, but I just don't have the strength."

"Betty would probably do anything asked of her," Emmie said. "I'd help more if we were staying here."

"I'd love to have you, Em, but you know there's no room for you and Bob."

"Anyhow, Betty wouldn't charge us an arm and a leg," Emmie said. "She'd do it for nothing, just because it's Sid."

"I'd prefer not to discuss that woman's relationship with my husband," Mary said. "I'm going to my room. Emmie, help Wendy with the dishes."

"You could afford a maid or a housekeeper, you know, Mother."

"And I don't want any more discussion about what I can or can't afford," Mary said fiercely. "Just get on with it." She glided out of the dining room, ramrod straight, and that was the end of it.

"She's losing it," Emmie said. "Thank God we're not trapped in this house. Although I guess I am until Bob gets back. Siddie, we've got to get Father away for good."

"It's being handled," Junior said.

A few hours later, when everyone had gone to bed and Emmie was in the upstairs TV room, dozing over a creaky old black-and-white movie, the front door opened quietly and a figure in an overcoat entered the dark foyer. Emmie had left the door unlocked, but had turned out all the lights on her way upstairs. The person fumbled along the foyer, feeling the walls to find the way, and reached the stairs. The sound of the television set caused the person to freeze in the act of mounting the stairs. Then the figure backed away and was out the door.

"Bob, is that you?" Emmie had come to the head of the stairs and was peering down into the gloomy foyer. "Damn! I was sure I heard . . ." Emmie returned to the movie, and Bob appeared an hour later to take her away, cross and sleepy.

"I don't like the looks of that car down there in front of the house," Bob said as they settled into his car, which he'd managed to get to the top of the icy driveway Betty hadn't dared attempt. "It was parked there when I left earlier and it's still here. Isn't street-parking overnight against the law hereabouts?"

"Somebody's engine wouldn't start," Emmie said. "So, how did your 'business' go?"

"Not as well as I'd hoped," Bob said.

Betty couldn't get to sleep after the card game, after her difficult day. She lay under the covers and listened to Cora and Dave's going-off-to-bed noises, and when the apartment was finally silent, sleep still didn't come. She missed the lump of Tina's feline weight against her thigh and the distant rumble of the furnace, even the sound of the occasional passing car on Timberhill Road.

She closed her eyes but kept seeing Sid, frail and incapacitated, with only his eyes truly alive. The eyes and the grip of his hand. She remembered the orchid she'd brought to Sid, standing bravely in the corner of his sickroom, and that reminded her of poor Mr. Takahashi, dead on the floor of his greenhouse, surrounded by his beloved plants.

She also kept imagining Bennie Mallis lurking outside the Edwards & Son offices that afternoon, and perhaps now in the parking lot, watching the apartment complex. At least she had the safe-deposit key safely in her handbag, waiting to be used to unlock who knew what. It was away from the office, so there would be no chance that Siddie would be hovering over her shoulder as she emptied the files on Monday, seeing her come upon it.

Suddenly she sat up in bed and turned on the little bedside lamp. Mr. Takahashi, likely murdered by his own son-in-law. Was Tommy really so stupid as to think the police wouldn't suspect him immediately, even with

Miho's denial that he wasn't the man she saw? And Siddie and the key. It would have been so easy for him to find it himself. Had he not looked, or was he not bright enough to think of the K file as the right and obvious place? That was another stupid thing—to let her do it, instead of doing it himself. On the other hand, by allowing her to find the key, which she had a right to use, perhaps he stood a better chance of appropriating what might be in that deposit box.

She squeezed her eyes shut and thought again about Mr. Takahashi. If Tommy hadn't committed the murder, who else could it have been? Like Siddie, perhaps Tommy hadn't taken the easiest way and handled the matter of his father-in-law personally. She doubted he had a stooge like Betty to do his job for him, but still . . .

She began to turn over the "what ifs" that flowed through her mind, and then she came to Arnie Harris. She would contact him in the morning. The thought of the jovial and sensible old friend helped her relax; she started to drift into sleep. Tomorrow was another day, and it would be better than today.

In the distinguished white colonial on the top of a hill in Wethersfield, the television set was dark and silent; Sid Junior and his wife had retired to the room they had grudgingly agreed to make their own after his father returned and needed the master bedroom. Before going to her own room, Mary Edwards had visited her husband in the big bedroom as he lay in his hospital bed. She had patted his hand, although he slept and was not aware of her presence, and then she had fled the room, close to holding her breath so as not to smell the odors of illness

that pervaded it. The Edwards grandchildren crept fairly
quietly into the house not long after their aunt Emily and
uncle Bob had departed, and had gone to their rooms—
not so quietly—so that their mother and father knew
they were home and not careening along icy roads with
possibly unsavory companions. Soon all the occupants
were asleep, and the house, too, slept in darkness.

It was Wendy who heard the noise through her sleep
and was instantly awake.

"Sid," she hissed. "Wake up."

"Whaaa?"

"I heard something. There's somebody in the house."

"There're half a dozen people in the house," Sid Junior
said groggily.

"I'm scared. Go look."

"Me? If someone's stealing my mother's silver, I don't
want . . ."

"The noise was upstairs," Wendy said, "I'm sure of it.
Out in the hall. Your mother doesn't keep her silver upstairs. At least she never did. Besides, I put it away
downstairs myself after dinner tonight. Maybe your father fell out of bed or something. We have to check on
him. I'll go with you. Please."

"Jeez, Wendy. One of the kids just went downstairs for
a Coke, or Mother went to the bathroom. Maybe you
heard Em and Bob leaving, or you were dreaming. It's
nothing." But he was awake now, sitting on the edge of
the bed, his feet on the floor. And listening.

But they did not bother to go out to the hall and look in
on Sid Edwards, nor did they check to see if someone
was stealing Mary Edwards's silver flatware that Wendy
herself had carefully washed and dried after dinner that

evening. Instead, they lay back on their pillows and soon fell asleep again, so they didn't hear footsteps on the pink-carpeted staircase—or the front door opening cautiously. No one saw a person get into the black car parked just up the street from the Edwards house, or saw the car roll silently down the street. No one heard the engine start finally as the car reached the cross street. Then the car drove away slowly, between the banks of snow piled up by the snowplows, and headed toward a small industrial city in the middle of Connecticut, where one friendly bar remained open for regulars only.

CHAPTER 15

IT WAS Mrs. Potter's scream that woke the Edwards household on Sunday morning. She stood in the hallway at the top of the stairs and shrieked and shrieked, until Sid Junior and Wendy had stumbled from their room while the teenaged Edwards children peered out behind half-opened doors.

"What the hell is going on?" Sid was not amused by being abruptly wakened by a hysterical woman. He briefly contemplated slapping her briskly, but fortunately she quieted at the sight of him, although she continued to breathe heavily, as though a war between sobs and simple breathing was going on in her chest.

"Is it Father Edwards?" Wendy asked. "Is he . . . ?"

Mrs. Potter gulped and managed to shake her head.

"Then what is it?" Sid spoke deliberately, then turned his head and spoke over his shoulder. "You kids go back into your rooms. Nothing to see here."

The children obeyed quickly. Wendy went to Mrs. Potter and put an arm around her. "What's the matter? Now, just calm down, and explain."

Mrs. Potter flapped her hands in the direction of the

closed doors lining the hallway. "Mrs.—Mrs.—" She gulped again and the tears began.

"Mother!" Sid flung open the door to Mary Edwards's bedroom, took a step inside, and backed out quickly. "Wendy, call an ambulance. Now. Mother's had a stroke. Or something."

Wendy retreated quickly to their bedroom and a phone.

Sid returned cautiously to his mother's room and was back in the hall by the time Wendy returned from her call.

"What happened, Sid?"

"Maybe Mrs. Potter can explain," Sid said.

"I—I just went in, and there she was, sprawled out on the bed. I panicked. She looked so awful."

"As well she might. She's dead, Wendy—and if I'm not mistaken, she's been strangled." Sid eyed Mrs. Potter. "That's all you have to say? You just went in and found her? Since when do you go into my mother's room without an invitation? You should be looking after my father."

"I looked in on him," Mrs. Potter said, "like I always do when I come in every morning. He was still asleep. I always check with Mrs. Edwards after I've seen him, and ask if I can bring her up some tea or coffee." She opened her mouth to say something more and failed to close it. Finally she said, "You don't think I had anything to do with—with that? If you do, I'm giving notice this second. For that matter, you two were here all night—and I know what I hear around this place . . . the money belonging to her and Mr. Edwards and the company. You know the old man is going to die sooner rather than later, and it's only her that stood to live a good long time—"

"That's enough," Sid said, with not-well-suppressed fury. "How dare you suggest anything of the sort! Wendy, you'd better call the police, too!"

"I told you I heard something in the night," Wendy said. "I told you. But you wouldn't look, no. And now see what's happened."

"Call," he said sternly. And to no one except the ceiling, he said, "Who did this? Why Mother?"

Mrs. Potter said, "She was a strong-willed old lady, like they had in the old days. No nonsense, and no fooling her. Somebody thought they could get away with something."

"That will be quite enough, Mrs. Potter. Kindly look after my father—see that he has his breakfast, and is settled for the day. Things are going to be difficult for the next few hours. Do not inform him of my mother's death, under any circumstances. I will speak to him later, after the authorities and medical help arrive."

"Poor old man should know right away that his wife has been strangled in her bed," Mrs. Potter mumbled. "It's only right."

"I decide what's right in this house, in this company. You will do what I say."

"Yes, sir," Mrs. Potter said, and opened the door to Sid Senior's bedroom. "Good morning, sir. I see you're awake. And doesn't that flower look pretty this morning . . ." She closed the door behind her.

Before Sid could think of much else to rant about, there was a frantic ringing of the doorbell downstairs. Wendy flew from their room, hair combed and robed in elegance.

"The ambulance or the police," she said as she raced downstairs.

Then they came upstairs, heavily and seriously. The medical people went into Mary Edwards's room, and the portly and somewhat sleepy policeman tried to get information from Sid.

"I don't know what happened. My father's caretaker, Mrs. Potter, found my mother when she came in this morning. She's in there with Dad now. He's had a stroke, is not well at all." Sid put his hands to his face. "This is a nightmare—as if I didn't have enough to worry about. My mother . . . murdered. And in her own house."

"I've got crime-scene fellows coming to check for fingerprints and such," the policeman said. "You know nothing about all this?"

"My wife thought she heard something in the night. It woke her up. But we didn't look; I couldn't imagine . . ."

"Very hard to imagine something like this happening, sir," the policeman said. "You didn't touch anything?"

"I—I may have touched the knob on the door. I went in and looked at her, felt for a pulse. I saw the wire or whatever around her neck, but it was dark. I didn't turn on the light or anything. I came out and told my wife to call an ambulance. And then the police."

"This Potter woman . . . She been with you long?"

"Since my father returned from Arizona after his stroke. She came highly recommended."

"He didn't change his will or anything of the sort after she took over?"

"Of course not. He can't speak, can't move, and I scarcely think he's developed a deep emotional attachment to that old cow, however competent."

"Well, my lad, I do have to ask. And who else was in the house last night?"

"My sister and her husband were here until . . . perhaps midnight. He was out and came back to pick her up. They're staying at a hotel not far away. My two children came in some time after midnight. They're in their rooms now, but they don't know anything about this."

"Anybody else been around—unusual people, I mean to say?"

"Well," Siddie said slowly, "my father's former office administrator, from before he retired last year, dropped by to see him. They were always very close."

"Nothing personal against your mother, though."

"I shouldn't think so, although my mother never took kindly to their closeness. They had a business relationship that Mother didn't or couldn't participate in."

"And where might I find this lady assistant?"

"I believe she's staying with friends in the Hartford area. I spoke to them last night when they called looking for her when she was late returning. I don't really know where . . . Her name is Betty Trenka. She's expected at our offices on Monday to help with clearing out my father's files. We left that for some time after he retired a few months ago, and then he had his stroke, and eventually came back here. We've been talking about putting him in a nursing home. My mother can't . . . couldn't care for him. Hence, Mrs. Potter."

"So if none of you murdered your mother . . ."

"I object to that suggestion—"

"What I mean to say is, since none of you committed murder, someone must have come into this house last night. Is that possible?"

"I'm sure my sister locked the door behind her when she left. She's responsible that way. The children have their own keys, but the door would have locked behind them."

"We'll be looking to see if someone broke in."

"No one broke in," Sid said. "This is a well-built, secure house."

"But if someone had a key . . ."

Sid looked at the ceiling above the policeman's head. "A key, yes. But who?"

"How about your Miss Trenka, your father's assistant?"

"Marginally possible, but highly unlikely. They kept their relationship away from the family."

"But there was a relationship—more than employer and employee? Pretty young thing who turned your father's head, perhaps?"

Now Sid laughed. "That doesn't describe Betty Trenka. She's nearly my father's age. A big lumpish woman with nothing of the siren about her at all."

"Nevertheless, I'd be grateful for a way of locating her."

"I wrote down the number of the people she's staying with," Sid said, "in case something happened to her on the way home, and we found out. It's probably downstairs."

"Well then, that's simple. You give me the number and you're out of it . . . Ah, this must be the crime-scene boys. You and the wife and kiddies just keep to your rooms until we're finished. My condolences on your mother's death. We'll figure it all out."

"Funny," Sid said, "it was always Father we expected would die first."

"Sometimes things don't work out as planned," the policeman said. "Come upstairs, boys. And mind you, don't track mud on that nice carpet."

Wendy trailed the police experts upstairs. "There's coffee if anyone wants it," she said. "Mrs. Potter has risen to the occasion— Sid, I told you someone was in the house, I told you."

"Calm down, Wendy. Everything's going to be okay. Could you—would you tell Dad? He might take it better coming from you."

Wendy closed her eyes briefly. "I guess I could. Better me than Mrs. Potter. But it will kill him, Sid. She's all he had."

"He still has Betty," Sid said. "Unless she murdered Mother."

CHAPTER 16

BETTY AND the Welleses went off together to early mass on Sunday morning. Betty was not yet prepared to participate fully in the ritual, but she felt a special need for the comfort of the familiar and the opportunity for a heartfelt prayer, surrounded by worshipers and the spiritual communion of the service.

After church, they stopped for a pancake breakfast at a restaurant near the apartment, and after a leisurely hour, during which Betty recounted some of her adventures in her new home, with Tina figuring more dramatically than in real life, they made their way back so that Betty could call Arnie Harris before the day had grown too old.

A policeman was at the door before they'd scarcely hung up their coats.

"Betty Trenka here?" The policeman was young and a bit nervous.

"I'm Betty Trenka. What's wrong?"

"Nothing wrong, exactly, ma'am. We just have a few questions."

"Please, come in," Betty said, and looked around to see Cora and Dave looking doubtful but nodding their agreement.

"It's about Mrs. Mary Edwards," the policeman said. "Do you know her?"

"I've known her for years," Betty said, "although I haven't seen her for several months—not since I retired from her husband's company."

"You didn't see her yesterday when you visited her home in Wethersfield?"

"No," Betty said, "but I understood she was resting while I was there to see her husband, my former employer. He's been quite ill, and as I was visiting my friends here, I thought— Is Sid all right?" She fought off a sudden clutch of fear.

"According to his son and the lady who looks after him, he's fine."

"But you said something about Mary. Is she all right?"

"I'm afraid there's bad news there. It appears that Mrs. Edwards died in the night."

"Died? What? How?"

"That's what we're looking into. Mrs. Edwards was apparently strangled some time during the night . . ."

"No! Does Sid know? Who did it?"

"Ah, that's the question we're all wondering about. Now where might you have been last night?"

Betty had been accused of a few things in her lifetime, but never anything like this. She was a respectable, hardworking woman of substantial years, and she wasn't prepared to be bullied by a copier salesman, the Internal Revenue Service, or a policeman young enough to be her son.

"I hope you aren't suggesting that I had anything to do with this," she said, as calmly as possible. She remembered that copier salesmen and policemen—and even the

IRS—didn't take kindly to belligerence, or even out-raged respectability. "In any event, I was right here with my friends. We had dinner after I returned from visiting Mr. Edwards in Wethersfield, then we played cards. We even spoke to the security men for the building because we noticed a suspicious person hanging about outside in the parking lot. I went to bed quite early after a busy day, and we went to church this morning."

"That's it? You didn't go anywhere last night?"

"No. My car is parked in Space Fifty-one, and hasn't been moved since I got back here from Wethersfield. The snow started to thaw a bit yesterday afternoon, so perhaps if you are really suspicious of me, you could tell that it hasn't moved out of the space since the afternoon thaw and the slight freeze that occurred at around nightfall."

"We're not suspicious, ma'am," the young policeman said kindly. "We're just trying to place everybody, so we can figure out who got into the Edwards house late last night and strangled the lady."

"Strangled." Mr. Takahashi had been strangled. In the night. Because he had apparently stood in the way. But what had poor Mary Edwards stood in the way of? It would be much more logical to strangle dear Sid, who stood in the way of Siddie and Emmie.

"Are you sure it wasn't a mistake? I mean, Mr. Edwards was more likely— Never mind. This news has made me feel a bit faint. Would you mind if we left this until later or tomorrow? Tomorrow I will be at Edwards and Son's offices in Grafton on a special project. You can find me there. Mr. Edwards Junior will confirm my business at the company—unless his mother's death changes his plans."

The young policeman grimaced and said, "Okay. You won't leave the area?"

"If I do, young man, it will be to return to my home in East Moulton. But I do not intend to leave here until Wednesday. In any event, Mr. and Mrs. Welles here have my home address and telephone number. The resident state trooper in East Moulton knows me. You could check with Officer Bob, and he will assure you, as I do, that I am a harmless, nonmurderous senior citizen who is sincerely devoted to Mr. Edwards and his entire family." That stretched a point when it came to Junior, so it wasn't strictly true, but the policeman seemed to find it acceptable. The policeman retired graciously, and Cora and Dave rushed to Betty's side.

"How awful." Cora was close to tears. "People breaking into a house that way and killing someone. Oh, Betty! It could have been your Sid who died that terrible way instead of his wife!"

"I think," Betty said thoughtfully, "that it should have been Sid. Maybe the wrong person got murdered."

"A mistake? Ha!" Dave, for one, wasn't convinced. "Things like that don't happen. Besides, even a dumb criminal knows the difference between an old lady and a paralyzed old man."

"Mmm." Half of Betty's mind was far away; the other half was organizing the things she had to do, the questions that needed answering. Had Siddie told his father about his mother? How had Sid taken the news? Was he going to be safe there in that house? She was increasingly certain that someone—Siddie or Emmie or even Bob Ruin—had hatched a plot to do away with Sid Edwards Senior, and that plot had somehow gone wrong. And how could anyone prove it? None of the three had the guts to do the deed themselves, so someone had been persuaded or hired to strangle Sid in his bed. A dumb criminal who made a mistake in his victim.

Then she was jolted by the picture of Bennie Mallis outside the Edwards & Son offices. A dumb criminal to be sure—someone Junior had been talking to behind closed doors at the company on Saturday afternoon while she was looking through the files.

"I have to call Arnie," Betty said. "And Junior."

It took a while for the phone at the Edwards house to be answered, and when it was, the very young voice suggested that it was one of Sid's grandchildren, the girl, whose name Betty had forgotten. "I'd like to speak to your father," Betty said. "This is Elizabeth Trenka."

"He's, like, pretty busy. My grandmother . . . died." Betty caught a hint of tremulous emotion in the girl's voice. At least someone in the household was having a normal reaction to the death.

She heard the girl call from the phone, "Daddy, it's that woman of Granddad's . . . Betty Trenka."

So that is how I am known, Betty thought. That woman of Granddad's, indeed!

"Look, Betty, I don't have time to chat. We've got a real problem here." Siddie was abrupt.

"I know, Sid. I heard about your mother," Betty said gently. "I'm so sorry."

"How the hell could you have heard? Is it on the news already?"

"The police told me. They just left. They knew I'd been at your place yesterday, and they were checking to see if I noticed anything. Is your father taking it well? I mean, as well as can be expected?"

"He hasn't been told. Mrs. Potter has been sworn to silence. The doctor is afraid that the shock might cause another stroke that would kill him. Emmie and Bob just got here, and they and Wendy and I are going to sit down and decide how to handle it." There was silence on the line for a moment. "Betty, my first instinct would be to have you handle it. I'm sure the others would agree. You know how to deal with my father; he's always relied on you, trusted you. You would know what to say."

"I think, Sid, that it should come from a member of the family, don't you?"

"And what are you? Don't you know that I know everything about you and Dad? An unlikely office romance, certainly, but I know he cared about you—probably more than he cared about my mother—and you certainly loved him. Please, tell him. Em and I can't do it. And besides, we've got a lot of things to deal with—the funeral, what to say to people, the police. What we're going to do with Dad now that Mother is gone. And the kids are in bad shape. I have to look out for them. Please. For old times' sake."

Sid Junior had never been a beggar, but he was begging now. She wondered if there was an element of guilt involved, since her number one suspect for arranging the murder had to be Junior himself.

"All right," Betty said finally. "I will handle it personally. When would you like me to come?"

"Around noon? Mrs. Potter is getting him set for the day. Mother always went in to see him in the morning, but I told Mrs. Potter to tell him that she had come down with the flu, and didn't want to risk passing it on to him. If he understands her, he won't worry if she doesn't show up today."

"He'll understand," Betty said. "He understands pretty much everything. And Sid, we can talk about this later, but will you want me to go ahead with clearing the files tomorrow as planned? I'd understand if you wanted to cancel."

"No!" Sid said quickly. "We'll get on with it. Very important. There's stuff in there I need, especially now that Mother is gone."

Betty couldn't resist one parting shot. "And I suppose Bennie Mallis will be around?"

"Bennie? Sure, he'll probably be around. He's back on the payroll. Look, you know that Dad never liked him, so don't mention him when you're here. It would only upset Dad."

"I'll be there around noon," Betty said. She looked in her handbag for Arnie Harris's phone number—and came upon the key she'd found in the files and Sid's note.

Sophie Harris assured her that Arnie was eager to talk to her. "He's taking the trash out for me; he'll be right in." It sounded as though Sophie put her hand over the mouthpiece to call out to Arnie. "Arnie! It's Betty Trenka. Don't track snow all over my nice carpet." To Betty, she said, "The thaw has set in and the streets are running with water. Here he is."

"Betty! Was I surprised to hear that you'd called yesterday. So, what can I do for you?"

"Quite a lot, Arnie. I need information. Is there some

time today when we could meet? I understand you're still part-time with Edwards and Son."

"Unlike you, me they can't do without." Arnie chuckled. "But it's not like the old days, with Senior there and you, things running like clockwork."

"Arnie, you probably haven't heard, but something happened to Mrs. Edwards last night."

"Kiddo, nothing happens to Mary Edwards that she doesn't plan. So what?"

"She was murdered. At home in Wethersfield. Someone came in during the night and strangled her."

"Such a thing!"

"I know. It's hard to believe. I have to go over there at noon to tell Sid Senior. Siddie doesn't want to do it, although I think he should be the one. Sid's not in good shape."

"So Junior was saying yesterday. I had to meet him at the office. I didn't understand what he wanted. He can look at the books himself perfectly easily. He says you'll be working on the files tomorrow, true? We'll talk then."

"I'll be there tomorrow, but I'd rather talk when there's no chance of Siddie overhearing. Maybe this afternoon?"

"Sophie and I are going to my son's house for dinner."

"It's really important, Arnie. Remember telling me to look under *K* for key?"

"Ha! You remembered that?"

"Well, I found it. I stopped at the office on Saturday on my way here. I don't know what to do about it, and you're the only person I can ask. Could we maybe meet there around three or four today? I still have the key to the front door. Arnie, I need your help."

"Okay, okay. You got it. As long as I get away in time for dinner. My son's wife is a nervous cook, plans everything down to the last second."

"And, Arnie . . . I noticed that Bennie Mallis is back."

"Lowlife. Yeah, Junior sticks with the quality. I don't leave anything lying around that Bennie might like to borrow, if you know what I mean. He's not a good example of rehabilitation by way of the prison system. You wait for me in my office—you remember where. I'll try to be there by three-thirty."

After she hung up, Betty went off to the kitchen, where Cora and Dave were drinking coffee and discussing the thaw. The piles of snow around the parking lot were already diminishing, and melted snow had gathered in puddles between the parked cars.

"Don't include me in your lunch plans," Betty said. "I have to go over to Wethersfield and—and tell Sid about Mary. Junior wants me to."

"Now, isn't he the brave boy—bringing in an outsider to do his job! Not that you're an outsider, Betty. But you know what I mean." Cora was contrite.

"I told him that I thought he should be the one," Betty said, "but he wants me to do it." She slumped down in a chair and Cora placed a mug of coffee in front of her. "I can't help thinking that Siddie had something to do with the murder of his mother. His parents were in his way."

"Maybe that's why he can't look his father in the eye to tell him," Dave said. "And if what you think is true, I wonder how safe the old fellow is!"

"But you have to eat," Cora said. "Dave and I were

planning to try the new seafood restaurant that just opened up off Silas Deane Highway."

"I'll pick up a sandwich somewhere," Betty said. "Somehow, I don't think I'll feel a lot like eating after I see Sid."

CHAPTER 17

THE SUN was trying to break through the clouds, and here and there patches of blue were visible. It had warmed up markedly, so that it was almost the temperature it had been before the snow, before Betty had even opened that infernal Federal Express letter from Sid Junior.

As she drove toward Wethersfield, she tried to think how Sid's situation should be handled now that Mary was gone. Mary hadn't participated much in his care, but she had been a continuing presence. Wendy and Junior wouldn't want to be left alone with him and Mrs. Potter, who was probably a very expensive proposition. Sid was wealthy enough to be able to afford a nice nursing home—and if necessary, Betty would take it upon herself to look at some for the family. He might be willing to go if she promised she'd be with him as much as possible.

It was as though a switch had been flipped. She'd spent the months since her retirement wondering how she could find a new focus for her life after Edwards & Son, and suddenly she had one. She certainly couldn't bring Sid into her home to live, but she could at least devote

153

her time and energy to his well-being at whatever location he found his place.

Yet one problem remained: Exactly how was she to tell him about Mary?

The Edwards house had a closed look. The curtains were all drawn, as though the inhabitants had gone away. A police cruiser was parked up the street, and there were two cars at the top of the steep driveway, probably Junior's and Bob Ruin's.

The door was opened promptly at her ring by Emmie. She looked as though she'd been crying. "Betty, you don't know how much we appreciate . . ."

"It's all right," Betty said. "It will be far easier for me to say the words, although they won't sound any better to him coming from me."

"Do you want to go up right now? We've had police around all night, and the medical people, but they say they're finished for the moment, anyhow. I had Mrs. Potter tell Dad that Mother came down with some kind of stomach flu in the night, to explain all the comings and goings in the hall."

"Siddie mentioned that story, so he wouldn't be concerned when he didn't see Mary in the morning." Betty put her shoulders back. "Let's get it over with."

The two women mounted the stairs, and Betty followed Emmie into Sid's room.

"Dad, look who's here again to see you."

Sid was lying propped up on pillows on the bed, but there seemed to be a smile in his eyes when he saw Betty.

"Join us downstairs before you leave," Emmie said. "We've got things to talk over." Then she said in Betty's ear, "Mrs. Potter is in her room. If he reacts badly to your news, give a shout and she'll be right with you. She's been warned."

Betty heard the door close, and said to Sid, "The orchid looks lovely, doesn't it? I hope Mrs. Potter knows how much water to give it. I'll remember to tell her about its care before I leave." She pulled up a straight chair and placed it beside the bed, then she took his hand, so he could answer yes or no easily with squeezes. "Are you feeling okay today?" Yes. "That's good." She held his hand hard and said, "Sid, I have some bad news." She saw the look of alarm in his eyes. "It's Mary. She's had an accident, and she didn't make it." Now his grip was like a vise, and she felt the two squeezes that meant no.

"I'm afraid it's true, Sid. Siddie and Em asked me to tell you because they're rather upset themselves. Please, just relax. Everything's going to be all right. I'll see that you're taken care of." She saw the questioning frown on his face—and knew that he was asking what had happened.

"It's a bit of a mystery," she said. "Apparently someone got into the house in the night, and—and killed her. No one knows why. The police are looking into it." Sid looked pale to her, and tragically sad. "I know it's terrible, almost too terrible to take in."

Yes, he signaled. And then he seemed to be trying to speak, but the look of concern on his face was almost more eloquent than words. "Mmmme." He finally managed to get that one syllable out. Me. Like Betty, he thought of himself as a better target for murder than Mary.

"There is no reason to think it was you they were after," Betty said. "It must have been a burglar who stumbled into Mary's room by accident, and when she was awakened, he panicked and killed her. I understand it was quick, so she didn't suffer."

Sid was clearly agitated now, and Betty steered the conversation, such as it was, in a different direction. "I finally spoke with Arnie Harris this morning. I thought that as long as I was in the neighborhood, it would be nice to see him, and you told me to talk to him about the key, remember?" She felt his grip relax a bit. "Remember how well Arnie handled the books? And that time we had an audit and he left the IRS guys speechless because everything was in such perfect shape? I'll never forget the expression on those guys' faces." She was casting about for other topics. "It's turned quite warm today, and all the snow is melting. We'll be seeing spring before you know it. I'm going to be around for a few days, clearing the files. I mentioned that yesterday. So I'll be seeing you, almost every day." Sid was no longer holding her hand tightly, but seemed to have fallen asleep.

She went to the door to Mrs. Potter's room and knocked gently. "He's sleeping, I think," she said when Mrs. Potter opened the door. "I told him about Mary, and he seemed to take it calmly, but he may start thinking about it later and get upset."

"Can you imagine murder happening in this house?" Mrs. Potter shook her head. "I can't. Mary Edwards took everything one step at a time, and always knew what was what, what she wanted. I tell you, Miss Trenka, those kids better decide what they're going to do with the old man, because they're close to seeing the last of me. I don't want to be spending my nights in a house where a body can get murdered in her bed."

"I hope you'll stay on until they do decide," Betty said.

"I don't think Emmie or Wendy could manage without you . . . Well, we're going to talk about what to do now."

"Tell the truth, Miss Trenka, you ought to be the one to make the decision, and stick to it. A nursing home would be the best, in my opinion. I've had cases like this before, and pretty soon the family loses interest and the patient doesn't get any attention at all. You should talk to the local visiting nurse. She comes here once a week to check on Mr. Edwards, make sure he doesn't have bed-sores and has the right medications on hand. She'll know all the right places for him. I got her number here some-where . . . Ah, here it is. You talk with this Mrs. McCal-lum. A real nice woman. That bunch downstairs wouldn't think to ask her. She's too much like a servant in their eyes."

Betty took her leave of Mrs. Potter, clutching the tele-phone number of the visiting nurse.

All the Edwards family members were sitting in the living room, and looked up expectantly as Betty arrived. Even the teenagers were there, looking unhappy and scared. Like every other room in the house, the living room was excruciatingly tasteful. Williamsburg blue walls, white drapes, subdued chintz upholstery on comfort-able furniture, fine golden sconces with low-wattage light bulbs, a Stiffel lamp or two, a gilt-framed mirror, a few more landscapes like those lining the staircase.

Betty looked around at them. "I told him about Mary. He was disturbed, of course, but he took it all right. Mrs. Potter is keeping watch in case he gets upset later, after thinking about it. Now . . ." Betty selected a comfortable armchair and sat. "We . . . you have to make some decisions about Sid's living situation. I'm not sure

Mrs. Potter is willing to stay on indefinitely, and I'm also not sure if you, Emmie, or you, Wendy, are prepared to become Sid's principal and long-term caregiver." She saw Emmie and Wendy exchange looks. "I'm not sure, finally, whether Sid is safe here. I am not convinced that Mary's murder was intended." She found she was watching Siddie. "That is, the true victim might have been Sid."

"Ridiculous." Bob Ruin glared at her, head up, shoulders back. The perfect image of a defiant (guilty?) son-in-law, braving out an accusation.

"He's been a man of some importance in his industry over the years, he may have made enemies—although I certainly never knew of any. Junior would know more about the business currently than I do. But he's in a highly vulnerable state now."

"Bob's right," Junior said. "Dad had no enemies, and if there's a problem in business, it would be me rather than him that someone might try to get rid of."

"Oh, Sid, no." Wendy sounded distraught, and the children looked positively scared.

"Maybe I'm overstating the matter, but the fact is, Sid needs to be in a situation where he'll be safe and properly taken care of. With your permission, I intend to investigate nursing homes. I assume that he can afford the best."

Siddie nodded glumly, and even Emmie indicated her agreement.

"Then that's settled. I'll try to get the files in as much order as possible tomorrow so that I can begin my search at once. When is the funeral?"

"What funeral?" Emmie seemed confused.

"Mother's funeral," Sid said. "I have to check with the

police and the funeral director, but I think it will be Tuesday afternoon. Visiting hours at the funeral home tomorrow afternoon and evening. Mother would not want a big fuss made. You'll be there, of course, Betty."

"Perhaps I should be here with Sid," Betty said, "since he can't be there. We'll discuss it tomorrow when I'm at the office. Right now, I have to meet Arnie Harris at Edwards and Son."

"What for?"

"Arnie and I are old friends, Sid," Betty said. "Edwards and Son is convenient for both of us. And I assume Bennie Mallis will be around to keep an eye on us."

"Bennie's not a bad kid," Sid said. "Even if Dad couldn't stand the sight of him—and, of course, you'd take Dad's side. Bennie was even kind of Mother's pet for a while. I'd send him over here to fix things around the house that neither Dad nor I was able to handle. A little plumbing here, electrical work there. It's too bad he got himself in trouble with Dad and the law. I think Mother used to write to him in prison, and when he got out, he came back to Edwards and Son, and asked me to give him a break. Dad was already out in Arizona by then, so it didn't matter. He does a few odd jobs around the place."

"That explains it," Betty said.

"I don't want you starting on those files until I'm there," Sid said.

"I promise not to touch the files today," Betty said. She stood up. "I will be at the office at nine, Sid. And let me say to all of you how sorry I am about Mary." Emmie walked her to the door and got her coat.

"You don't really think someone's going to come back and try to kill Father, do you?"

"Not really," Betty said. "But be sure Wendy locks up carefully tonight."

Betty had to hurry to be on time to meet Arnie, so he could get to his son's house on schedule. There was no traffic to speak of on this Sunday afternoon, so she reached Edwards & Son in plenty of time. She again left her car parked in front of the building and tried the front door. It was unlocked, so she went in cautiously. The lights in the reception area were on, although she saw no one.

"Arnie! It's me!" Her voice echoed.

"And here I am," someone said, but it wasn't Arnie. A tall, muscular young man swaggered out of one of the offices—Sid Junior's, to be exact.

Betty stifled a gasp and commanded herself not to be afraid. It was Bennie Mallis. "Sid called and said you and the old bookkeeper were coming by, and he wanted me to be on hand to greet you. Greetings."

"Hello, Bennie. It's been a long time." But actually not very long, since she'd seen him the day before, and he'd seen her.

"Miz Trenka, is it true what Sid told me—that his mother was murdered?"

"I'm afraid so," Betty said.

"It shouldn't have happened," Bennie said. "She was an okay old dame. Stood by me through it all. What a stupid thing."

"Stupid things happen," Betty said, "when you least expect them. Is Arnie here yet?"

"Just me. You want to wait by his desk? You know the way."

"I do," Betty said. "When he comes, tell him where I am."

And a few minutes later, Arnie was there—a little grayer than she remembered, but with the same disheveled hair and the familiar big grin.

"So, Betty. You're looking good." He sat down in the big wooden office chair at his desk. "Take a load off, tell me what's up."

When Betty sat down, she was overwhelmed with weariness. "I don't know where to begin, Arnie. I told you I found the key to the safe-deposit box on Saturday, and papers that say which bank. Have you been paying for the box all along?"

He nodded. "Sid asked me to continue to handle his and Mary's personal bills. The box was a private matter, nothing to do with the company, so I kept up the quarterly payments. Now that Mary's gone and Sid's in bad shape, I probably can't anymore. Junior has been keeping an eye on everything I do. Sid definitely didn't want Junior to know about that box. But now that you have the key and all, you can open it. What's in it is yours."

"No, it's Sid's."

"Everybody seems to know about the box, but I kept my mouth shut."

"Everybody?"

"Well, I had Mary in here asking about it. Sid must have mentioned something to her. She didn't like the idea that you had one key and Sid had the other. Claimed whatever was there was hers."

"Was this after they got back? After Sid had his stroke?"

Arnie nodded. "I hardly ever remember Mary coming to the office, but one day I saw her here, talking to that no-goodnik Mallis. Then she got onto me, saying that Sid would be dead soon so the box and its contents were part of his estate, and in effect hers. I told her there was nothing I could do. You and Sid signed the papers. That drove her wild, I can tell you."

"Mary Edwards wild? Hard to imagine."

"But always a lady, just a mad one."

"So what should I do, Arnie? Go look at the box? There was this note with the papers . . ." She found Sid's note in her handbag. "It says, 'Things I've acquired for you.' What could he mean?"

Arnie shrugged. "I'll go with you, if you like. I know the girls at the bank. I can't be with you when you open the box, but if I can help in any way . . ."

"Thanks, Arnie. When do you work here?"

"Mondays, Wednesdays, and Fridays, mostly. I'll be here tomorrow afternoon. We could slip out to the bank before it closes."

"I don't like the idea of Bennie Mallis being around here. You know, if I were the suspicious type, I'd think Junior had persuaded Bennie to hasten his father's death, and Bennie opened the wrong bedroom door."

"Betty, Betty. Things like that don't happen. Besides, Bennie was crazy about Mary; he would have recognized her—and he wouldn't have hurt her."

"Someone did."

"Someone who didn't know her then." Arnie stood up. "I've got to get moving, but I'll see you tomorrow. You got any questions I can help with about the stuff in the files, let me know."

Betty was left alone in the familiar old building. She sat and thought for a while, and when she finally left, the lights in the reception area were off and Bennie Mallis was nowhere in sight.

CHAPTER 18

BETTY STOPPED at the reception desk and took a chance on calling Mrs. McCallum, the visiting nurse. She hated to bother her on a Sunday afternoon, but she wanted to get all possible appointments in place before she began her few days' work at Edwards & Son.

"My name is Elizabeth Trenka," Betty said, "and I used to work for Sid Edwards. I understand you look in on him regularly, and his caregiver, Mrs. Potter, suggested that you might help in recommending nursing homes."

"I know the ones in the area," Mrs. McCallum said.

"I don't mean that we should have a long telephone conversation now," Betty said. "I'm really sorry to be troubling you today, but I'm only in the area for a few days. Could we arrange to meet while I'm here?"

It was possible, so that was settled. Betty would see her on Wednesday.

"I'm surprised the family hasn't asked more questions," Mrs. McCallum said before she hung up. "They haven't been especially concerned about his needs, although I understood Mrs. Edwards was opposed to a nursing home."

164

"Mrs. Edwards died suddenly last night," Betty said. "An accident." It must have been an accident, Betty told herself.

"How terrible," Mrs. McCallum said, then added, "I should have thought that accidents ending in death were more likely to happen to Mr. Edwards. Forgive me, I shouldn't have spoken so, but I don't have a high opinion of the family's desire for him to get well and go on living."

"And how did Mrs. Edwards feel about that?" Betty asked.

"I'd rather not comment. I'll get some information together and see you on Wednesday."

Betty found a corner store near Cora and Dave's that made sandwiches, so she got one to take home, hoping they would be out somewhere. They were, leaving her a note that they'd gone to a movie that Dave had been dying to see.

Betty ate her solitary sandwich, found the iron, and did some unnecessary pressing of the suit she planned to wear the next day. Then she went to bed, and this time, she had no trouble going right to sleep.

It seemed very much like old times when Betty walked into Edwards & Son on Monday morning. She was almost the first person there, as she'd always been. The secretary arrived just behind her, an attractive young woman who was hugely pregnant.

"Hi, you must be the Miss Trenka Mr. Edwards has been talking about. I'm Linda, Mr. Edwards's secretary, but"—she patted her stomach—"I'm about to retire. Think of it—no more telephones, no more faxes, no more memos. Just a sweet little baby to play with all day long."

Although Betty had never been a mother, she was quite sure that life with a baby wasn't daylong playtime.

"If there's anything I can do to help, let me know," Linda said. "But, of course, you know your way around the place. Better than me, probably. Ah, here's Nan, the receptionist. Nan, meet Miss Trenka. You must have heard people like Arnie mention her. She worked here for practically forever."

"Hi," Nan said sullenly. Betty recognized her voice from her phone call to Sid.

"I remember when Miriam had your job," Betty said.

"She got fired," Nan said. "Mr. Edwards said he wanted to clean house, whatever that meant." Nan leafed through the appointment book on her desk. "Hey, Linda. Mr. Edwards is interviewing somebody for your job around noon."

"I heard," Linda called from Sid's office. "But maybe he won't come in. You heard about his mother, didn't you? Murdered in her bed over the weekend."

"No kidding? I'll just tell people he can't be reached until I hear from him." Nan looked at Betty wide-eyed. "Murdered? That mean old woman? I'd sooner see her doing the murdering."

"I don't think it would be wise to gossip openly about it," Betty said, and realized she was assuming a supervisory position that she didn't rightly hold. "I mean, if Mr. Edwards should hear you, it would only make it worse for him."

"Right, yeah. But what really happened?"

"An intruder, I understand. I really don't know much

about it," Betty said. "Well, I'd better get to work. Mr. Edwards wants the files in his father's office cleared out as soon as possible. Are there boxes and twine I could use?"

"Bennie probably has stuff. I'll ring him." She looked at her watch. "He's always late, but I'll find him, tell him what you need." Nan seemed to brighten considerably at the thought of contacting Bennie Mallis. He still had a gift for charming the young women of Edwards & Son.

Betty went into Sid Senior's office and switched on the lights. The filing cabinets loomed up like a row of soldiers. She started with *A*. The drawer was crammed with green hanging folders, crammed with manila folders, crammed with papers. She dropped a pile of folders on Sid's desk and sat down to go through them. In half an hour, the wastepaper basket was overflowing, and there was a small pile of glossy catalogs on the desk. Those she would tie up for recycling. In that time, she'd found perhaps an inch worth of paper possibly worth saving, some correspondence from customers that could be useful. By the time she got to the *B* drawer, she was knee-deep in discarded paper, and just about then, Bennie appeared with a couple of empty cardboard cartons and a role of twine.

"Thanks, Bennie. Could you manage to tie up that stack of catalogs? Is Mr. Edwards in yet?"

"Later," Bennie said. "Nan said he called and said he had to see the funeral director about his mother's funeral."

"Poor Mary," Betty said, and paused to watch Bennie's trembling hands attempt to tie up the bundle. "Is something wrong, Bennie?"

"Nothing," he said sharply. "I don't want to talk about Mrs. Edwards, okay?"

"Okay," Betty said. She continued to work steadily, still finding nothing of value, and Bennie hung around, tying up stacks of paper for her and carting out filled cartons. Near noon, she'd managed to get to the *G* drawer, and considered that she'd made good progress.

"Is that lunch place across the street still as lousy as ever?"

"You bet," Bennie said.

"Then I think it's time for me to see if they've kept up their standards for grilled cheese sandwiches." She wanted to be back when Arnie arrived.

"I'm meeting a guy myself in a couple of minutes," Bennie said. He swaggered out, and Betty followed.

Linda had taken over for Nan at the receptionist's desk, but clearly did not find the departing Bennie as attractive as Nan did. Junior was there, apparently just arrived, since he still wore his overcoat. "Ah, Betty. How are you getting on?"

"Making progress," Betty said. "I'm going to run across the street to get a sandwich."

"Good, good. I'll check in with you after lunch."

He headed for his office and Betty went to the front door.

She managed to contain her surprise at the sight of Miss Levenger, clutching her résumés and looking from Bennie Mallis to Tommy Crandell as they greeted each other.

"Miss Trenka! What are you doing here?"

"I might ask the same of you, Kathy. Actually, I'm here because I'm doing some work here this week."

"I've got a job interview. I tried to find you the other

day, but the kid who was feeding your cat said you were away."

At least Tina was getting her meals, and probably missed Betty not at all.

"You're interviewing here? At Edwards and Son?"

"Tommy fixed it up. He knows that guy who works here." She tossed her head in the direction of Bennie. "Some secretary is having a baby, and doesn't want to come back afterward. I said I wasn't really a secretary, but Tommy said it was more like a gal Friday job. I've got to start somewhere. At least the interview is good experience, don't you think?"

"I think—I think yes, you're right." But Betty was thinking about other matters. "Well, Mr. Edwards is here, so you'd better go in. You don't want to be late for your interview. Go right on in. Linda, the girl who's leaving, is at the receptionist's desk. She'll take care of you."

"Old friends, I see," Betty said as she passed Bennie and Tommy. "Hello, Tommy." The last time she'd seen Tommy was at the greenhouse, the day after Mr. Takahashi's murder. The one he didn't commit. Then she'd seen Bennie, prior to Mary Edwards's murder, which no one had yet said he committed. Slowly, very slowly, she began to put some pieces together. Tommy in prison for a previous attempt on Mr. Takahashi's life. Bennie in prison for stealing from Edwards & Son. Prison pals—so much so that Bennie fixed up an interview for Kathy, Tommy's friend. What else had been fixed up? And for what favored person?

"You know this dumbo, Miss Trenka?" Bennie was nonplussed.

"I know his wife, and knew his late father-in-law

slightly. I can't say I really know Tommy. I've got to get my lunch so I can get back to work."

Betty hurried across the street to the luncheonette, but felt the two men's eyes watching her. She turned slightly as she entered the steamy, noisy luncheonette—and saw the two of them conferring, heads together.

The counterman looked her up and down and beamed. "Back again, are you? I knew retirement wouldn't take."

"I'm still retired," Betty said. "I'm just here to clean up a mess or two."

"Grilled cheese and tomato, I'll bet," the counterman said.

"You never forget, do you?"

"Not me. What kind of messes? I hear the old lady, the wife of the boss, got killed. They ain't askin' you to solve the crime, are they? He peered through the steamed-up window. " 'Cause if they are, you start with Bennie Mallis. I seen him in here with Mrs. Edwards, drinking coffee and talking together like they was plotting the overthrow of the U.S. of A. Bet Mr. Edwards didn't know about that. He couldn't stand Mallis. But I hear he's real sick now. Too bad. I liked the guy; he was real decent."

"You saw Bennie and Mrs. Edwards talking in here often?"

"Past few weeks, yeah."

"Bennie's outside right now, talking to a big fellow. Ever seen them here?"

"Hey, you are crime-solving!"

"No, but that fellow has hooked up with a girl I know, and I don't think he's right for her."

The counterman peered out the window again. "Yeah,

I seen him around here with Mallis. And if they're best buds, you're right. He's nobody I'd want to see my daughter hanging with. Not Mallis, neither."

"I'll try to steer her away from him, and please don't mention to Bennie that I was asking about him. I don't want to get on his bad side."

"These lips are sealed. I wouldn't want him mad at me, that's for sure. He's a bad 'un."

"The grilled cheese was excellent, as always," Betty said. "It's nice to know that some things never change. I've got to get back to the office and finish up my work. I'm not as good at staying late as I used to be."

Bennie and Tom had gone when she emerged from the luncheonette. Nan was taking over the phones for Linda when she got back to the office.

"Is Kathy Levenger still being interviewed?"

Linda raised her eyebrows. "Hot little number, isn't she? You know her?"

"I helped her with her résumé, but I'm not sure she's up to doing the kind of good job you must have to do for Mr. Edwards."

Linda laughed. "Maybe he wants to catch them young and train them to his ways. Say, Arnie came in a couple of minutes ago. Asked for you. He's back in his office. And a Mrs. Welles called you—said you were staying with her and wanted you to call her about dinner."

Betty was feeling tired. Cora was a great one for dining out at places that had massive salad bars and lots of hanging plants, but Betty was more inclined toward a bowl of soup and bed. Her months of leisure had sapped her dedication to her work, and to socializing. But she wanted to get at least as far as the *J* file by the end of the day.

"Arnie, think we'll have time to run over to the bank?" He was hunched over his ledgers when she found him at his desk.

"It closes at three, so we'd better go now. The boss is talking to some pretty young thing who wants a job. Let's sneak out while we have the chance."

It wasn't far to the bank, but they took Betty's car, the better to avoid the increasingly deep pools of melted snow.

While Arnie settled himself into a chair outside the room where the boxes were stored, a young woman checked Betty's signature card, shuffled papers, and let her into the room.

"It's this one right here. You can put it on the table to look at the contents. Use your key to open it after I've used mine. Think you'll be long?"

"Not very. I just need to check some things."

The box was heavy and quite long. She lifted the lid and peered inside. A bundle of papers that looked like birth certificates and other official documents. There were no thick packets of currency, so the idea that the box was crammed with money was as foolish as it had sounded originally. She found a sealed manila envelope and was startled to see her name written across it in Sid's handwriting. She decided not to open it here but to take it with her. Quickly she looked through the rest of the contents. Stock certificates in Mary and Sid's names. A bankbook, which surprisingly did have her name on it, along with Sid's. She took that as well, without looking at the amounts. Bankbooks were pretty old-fashioned, so this one must date from years ago. She'd ask Arnie.

It took her only about fifteen minutes to finish, and soon she and Arnie were heading back to Edwards & Son.

"So?"

"No piles of cash. Only things that relate to me are an envelope and a bankbook. Like a savings bank used to give you." She took it out of her pocket and handed it to him. "Take a look."

He looked. "It's yours," he said. "These things don't pay much interest, but there's a couple of hundred thousand in the account."

"What?" Betty grasped the steering wheel so as not to run them off the road as she recovered from the surprise.

"All that money should be somewhere else making more money. On the other hand, I've got the interest statements for this account—they've been coming into the office. You haven't really earned all that much over the years, so maybe you won't have any big problem with the IRS over taxes."

"But where did the money come from?"

"Sid was probably putting it in for you over the years."

"He gave me money when we retired. He's going to need it himself if he ends up in an expensive nursing home."

"You can give it back if you want. He probably just didn't want Junior or Emmie to get their hands on it. Or Mary." He pointed to the envelope she kept on her lap as she drove. "You want me to look at that?"

"I think I'll wait and do it myself," Betty said. "I think it's a private thing between Sid and me."

They drove the short distance back to Edwards & Son in silence.

Finally Betty said, "I keep trying to figure out why

Mary Edwards was murdered. To be sure, she was sort of a barrier to the greed of her son and daughter, but I doubt that her death will make much difference in the long run. Here she is, a woman, quite social, but stuck with a husband who will never recover from his stroke. All the same, he's probably going to die fairly soon, and meanwhile, his care is costing a fortune. She probably feels she has no life of her own anymore, and she's feeling helpless—and this is a woman who's always been pretty much in charge of things. Strong-willed and all that. Now her so-called golden years have turned to lead."

Arnie frowned. "Maybe this woman also knows that over the years her husband has had someone he loves more than he loves her. It sounds as though she didn't have much to live for herself."

"My question is, could her greedy children have plotted to get rid of her first and then go on to getting rid of their father?"

"Betty, we've both known Siddie for years and years. He's not what you'd call a real nice person, but I can't imagine him murdering his parents. Can you?"

Betty shook her head. "But they're in his way. Arnie, just a few days ago, there was another murder. An old Japanese man . . . He was murdered in his greenhouse. I don't think they know who did it, but he, too, was standing in someone's way."

"Betty, Betty. Your imagination is running wild. That's not like you."

"I don't think my imagination is running anywhere," Betty said. "I think I know what must have happened."

"But can you prove it?"

"Not in a million years," Betty said. "But it's a comfort to think I know."

CHAPTER 19

WHEN THEY returned to the office, Betty asked Arnie to keep the bankbook in his possession, then she went to Sid's office, still littered with papers, boxes, and tied bundles of catalogs, and closed the door.

She placed the envelope she'd found in the safe-deposit box on the desk and sat down. She stared at the envelope for a while, imagining Sid sealing it and writing her name on it. She could tell by the feel of it that it didn't contain a stack of papers—rather that it was lumpy, as though it held several small boxes. Then she got out the letter from Sid she'd found in the *K* file, along with the key, and read it again: ". . . property of mine that belongs to you and you alone . . . things I've acquired for you, things I would have liked to have given to you before but could not . . . Love, Sid."

Finally she got up the courage to slit the sealing tape with the letter opener from a cup on the desk. She remembered the opener well. A thin silver blade with an elaborate key design on the end. She'd given it to Sid as a Christmas present perhaps twenty years ago. They never exchanged gifts, but she'd found the letter opener in a gift shop near Glastonbury, and had bought it because the

176

key made it so appropriate for the president of a lock-making company.

"Mmm. Nice," he'd said, and she'd been disappointed by his emotionless response to her present, but he'd kept it on his desk from that day to this. Brief tears stung her eyes at the memory, but then she dumped the contents of the envelope onto the desk. It was filled with boxes, some red leather tooled with gold, some dark blue velvet, even a couple of plain white cardboard boxes. There was also a square cream-colored envelope, so she untucked the flap and read the brief note, handwritten on a heavy square card:

> For all the holidays and birthdays that have passed without acknowledgment, from places I have visited without you, although you were always with me.

She picked up a slightly domed red box and pushed the button to open it. The overhead lights flashed back at her from the band of diamonds nesting in a slit in the velvet. On the inside of the box's top were the words "Kasliwal Jewellers Agra India."

"Oh, Sid," she said aloud. Then she whispered, "Thank you."

One of the blue velvet boxes held a gold bangle set with sapphires and diamonds. That box was marked with the name of a Bangkok jeweler. The next contained a string of luminous pearls from Japan. There was a huge, square-cut emerald ring he'd bought in South America, an exquisite and intricate necklace also from India composed of rubies, emeralds, and diamonds. A brooch in the shape of a parrot whose fierce eye must certainly be a yellow diamond, emerald earrings, another ring with a very deep blue heart-shaped stone. She searched her memory for its name.

"Tanzanite," she said out loud, but then she thought she heard someone outside the door and hastily swept the boxes into the top drawer of the desk, so that all were gone when Sid Junior opened the door.

"How are you getting on, Betty?"

"As far as *G*," she said. "I was hoping you were Bennie with more boxes for me."

"He's around here someplace," Sid said. "I'll send him along as soon as I see him."

"Did you hire Miss Levenger?"

"What?"

"The girl you were interviewing for Linda's position."

"Kathy. Well, no. She's a cute kid, but she really doesn't have much experience. In a small company like this one, you need someone who can do everything already and doesn't need training. You know her?"

"She comes from East Moulton. It's quite a coincidence, really. The fellow who came with her knows Bennie—so as a favor, Bennie got you to see her."

"That's not quite the case," Sid said. "My mother asked me to see her. And I could never say no to my mother." He actually looked briefly grief-stricken at mentioning her. "Of course, Bennie might have asked my mother to ask me—he's a first-class manipulator—and I told Mom a hundred times that he was nobody she should befriend, but she wouldn't listen to me. You know what he's like, his history. I find him useful, but that's no reason for a seventy-year-old woman to treat him like her best friend. Well, your Miss Levenger will have to seek employment elsewhere. I suppose if Mother were still alive, I'd be teaching the girl how to turn on the copier and how to tell callers I didn't want to speak to that I was out of the office at a business meeting. Well, I won't keep you from your work. Haven't found anything interesting yet, have you?"

"Nothing at all. I saved some correspondence from customers we've had for years—in case you wanted a complete history of our dealings—but the rest of the stuff is just paper."

"You didn't find any keys or the like."

"I don't think your father would feel the need to file away keys, since the factory is full of them."

"I meant keys that aren't like the ones we manufacture."

Betty shook her head. The idiot could have found the safe-deposit key himself with a little common sense.

"I hear you and Arnie took a little trip to Conn United this afternoon."

"How would you hear something like that?"

Sid shrugged. "I said I found Bennie useful."

Betty was grateful to Sid for turning on his heel and leaving her alone. She carefully returned the jewelry boxes to their envelope and set to work again on the files. Curiously, she hadn't found anything that resembled Emmie's "stuff" from her youth, and tried to think where Sid might have filed it. It hadn't been under *E* for Emily, or *C* for children, or even *F* for family. She had to assume that Emmie's request for help in retrieving her belongings was simply a tale contrived to give her a chance to look through the files, perhaps for the safe-deposit box key. She expected to see Emily in the office at any minute, but the afternoon passed, and she managed to reach her goal of getting through *J* by the day's end.

Bennie slouched in with more boxes, and Betty said, "I understand you're keeping track of my movements."

"I do what I'm told to do," Bennie said. "It's what they pay me for."

"Including murder?" Betty could have kicked herself for that unwise comment, to judge from the look on Bennie's face.

"I don't know what you think you know," Bennie said, "but if I were you, I'd forget it. Fast."

He left her somewhat shaken. The menace in his voice was quite serious.

In the course of the afternoon, she managed to call Cora, to assure her that she'd be back by dinnertime, that she probably wouldn't be going around to see Sid today.

"With Mary's death, I doubt that I would be welcome at the house today," Betty said. "They'll be having people in, I'm sure—and making arrangements for the funeral."

"A nice quiet evening at home is what you need," Cora said. "All this has been very stressful. Maybe . . ."

"A game of cards would relax me," Betty said. "I'll see you and Dave in a little while."

Junior appeared to have departed, and Linda and Nan were at the front door in their coats when Betty came to the reception area.

"See you in the morning," Betty said, as the young women departed.

Now she was alone in the building, as she used to be alone after hours for all those long years. This was the time when she used to get a lot of work done, without ringing phones and minor crises.

"Those days are over and done with," she said to the walls. "We are shriveling up and dying away." She looked down at the manila envelope she clutched to her chest, the gifts that Sid could not give her over the years—the ones that had to wait until life was ending. Only the bright fire of Sid's diamonds and the love she gave in return would burn through the years, outliving all of them.

The up-and-down weather had made a downward turn, and it was cold again. The puddles of melted snow had turned into little icy lakes. The spaces between the old cobblestones were filled with frozen rivulets that twinkled in the light of the streetlamps. Fortunately the engine of the Buick ignored the deep-freeze and roared to life.

As Betty drove carefully toward Cora and Dave's, avoiding the icy patches, she mentally organized what needed to be done in the next two days. She thought she could easily finish the files tomorrow; she had been to the bank and solved the question of the safe-deposit box. She was, she realized, quite well-off now, with the extra funds that Sid had set aside for her and the jewels— although she doubted they would have an extremely high value if she chose to dispose of them. But how could she do that? They represented, as Sid had written, all the holidays and birthdays over their thirty-seven years together. Well, extreme poverty might excuse their sale. She ought to have them valued for insurance purposes.

Then she pulled into a gas station, far away from the gas pumps, and opened Sid's envelope. She found the domed red box from the Indian jeweler, took out the band of diamonds, and slipped it on her finger. It fit perfectly, and somehow it made her feel at peace.

Elizabeth, you are not a jewelry person, she told herself sternly, but obviously gems had some sort of narcotic effect, and she wondered if by putting on the ring, she was on the road to addiction. She took a moment to look again at the jewelry in the other boxes. The emerald she put into one pocket of her coat, and the parrot with the yellow eye into the other. Then she found the tanzanite ring and slipped it into her pocket.

Betty did not at first notice the black car that had pulled into the gas station after her and sat idling near the brightly lighted office. She did notice it in her rearview mirror as it followed her when she moved out into traffic.

The car stuck close to her, even running yellow and red lights to stay behind her. Betty began to get worried, and could only think that it was Bennie and Tommy who were trailing her home. But why? Sid knew where she was staying, and she'd even left the address and Cora's phone number with Nan.

She didn't care at all for the idea of being involved in a car chase on the outskirts of Hartford. When the black car was finally stopped by a traffic light and heavy cross-street traffic, Betty speeded up a bit and made a quick right-hand turn onto a quiet residential street that she knew would eventually bring her back to the main road and into the center of downtown Hartford. No one was following her now, so she relaxed and drove on, coming to a halt at a stop sign on a corner.

The next thing she knew, the black car had come to a stop beside her and a man wearing a concealing ski mask was pulling open the door on her side of the car. Another man was opening the door on the passenger side. He grabbed Sid's envelope, which was lying on the seat, and slammed the door. The other man held on to Betty's wrist as she struggled to free herself. The diamond band reflected the lights on the dashboard, but apparently this wasn't a simple robbery. He didn't attempt to take it. Maybe he hadn't even noticed it. Then Betty found her wrist had been released and she saw the two men race to get back into their car and speed away.

Her heart was thumping, and she felt dizzy, but except for losing some of Sid's treasures, she was undamaged—although she mentally berated herself for not locking the doors as she drove, for not seeing the license plate on the black car, for not taking careful note of the two men. She would never be able to identify them, and despite her suspicions, she couldn't even be sure they were Bennie and Tom.

Had Junior put them up to this? Was he so desperate to see what she had gotten at the bank? At least Arnie had the bankbook, and the key was still tucked away in her handbag, along with Sid's two notes to her.

"I certainly hope I don't see Wendy Edwards wearing a sapphire and diamond bangle bracelet," she said. Then she shut her mouth. Talking aloud to herself was almost as unforgivable as talking to the cat.

She came limping home to Cora and Dave's—and was never so happy to see the lights on in a kitchen and the figures of her friends through the window, setting the dinner table and stirring a pot. But now she was angry, and there were a few things she planned to say to Junior in the morning. She'd better see that Sid was out of that house as soon as possible, since his son was apparently crazed.

"I'm back!" she called as she came through the back door from the parking lot.

"Are you all right?" Cora looked concerned.

"Why do you ask?" Betty felt all right, although her wrist throbbed a bit.

"You look—you look tired," Cora said weakly. "How about a glass of wine? Dave's just opened some."

"Maybe I will," Betty said. "I've had a rather interesting day."

When she'd told her tale, Cora said, "You must call the police at once."

Betty shook her head. "I don't think so. No way to identify them—and since they took only the envelope from the safe-deposit box, I have to think Sid Junior put them up to it."

Dave said, "I think Betty's right. It will just add to the trouble. It was probably those two stupid louts, hired by Sid Junior. Sort of like hit men."

Betty suddenly felt dizzy, and put her hands to her face.

"I see," she said. "Stupid hit men. Don't look so worried, Cora. I just solved a crime but I can't prove it. Not yet."

CHAPTER 20

CORA KNOCKED on Betty's door early the next morning. "Someone's calling you," she said. "A Mrs. Potter. Says it's important."

Betty was out of bed in a flash. Something had happened to Sid.

"Mr. Edwards is fine," Mrs. Potter said. "I wanted to catch you before you went to the office. Young Mr. Edwards won't be in today, because of the funeral. Could you come around and sit with Mr. Edwards Senior? He seems to want you."

"Of course, but how do you know that?"

"The old fellow and I understand each other pretty well. He kept pointing at that orchid thing you brought him, real agitated. So I asked him if it was you he wanted, and he let me know pretty clearly that it was. So you'll come? The funeral is at two, and I kinda wanted to go, seeing as Mrs. Edwards was the one who was paying me."

"I'll be there," Betty said. "Does one-thirty give you time enough to get to the funeral?"

"Fine," Mrs. Potter said. "Mr. Edwards will be pleased to see you. He's doing pretty well today, lots more movement in his right side, and he managed to say a few words I could understand."

Thank you, St. Jude, Betty said to herself. Then she rushed through dressing and breakfast, and made sure she had the diamond ring on one hand, the emerald on the other. Then she decided that the emerald was too much and put it aside. She tucked the book about strokes in her bag to read up about nursing homes before she saw Mrs. McCallum, and headed for Edwards & Son, and another day at the files.

It was mercifully peaceful throughout the morning, with no sight of Bennie and with Sid away handling matters relating to his mother's funeral. Arnie was not there, either, although he did call her and listened with horror to the story of her hijacking by the two men.

"I was sorry to lose the jewelry Sid had bought for me," she said, "but I managed to save a couple of pieces."

"Diamonds, what are they? Bits of carbon, same as charcoal. As long as you weren't hurt."

"Arnie, there can't be anything of value in the files. I expect to reach *S* in the next hour or two, and then I'm leaving to sit with Sid during Mary's funeral. I'll be finished here tomorrow. I'll see the visiting nurse about nursing homes, and then I'm gone."

"If you ask me, those files just hold Sid's business history."

"Oh, I did locate a business plan he worked up, something about a merger with another company. The way I read it, though, while somebody would make a little money—probably Sid and Emmie—Sid would be out of a job. No fancy office, no title, nothing. No more Edwards and Son."

"Sid mentioned his thoughts on a merger more than a year ago, before Junior forced him out, but he didn't want to let go of the company."

"I suppose I should hand it over to Junior and let him do what he wants with it. At least I have something to show for my work on the files."

She left the business plan on Junior's desk before leaving for Wethersfield.

The family had already departed for the service when she arrived, and she was greeted by Mrs. Potter in a solemn black dress and a remarkably perky little black hat.

"He's waiting for you," Mrs. Potter said. "I've got to run. I'll be back after the service. They'll probably be having people over, but Mrs. Edwards Junior has everything laid out nicely."

"Hello, Sid." He was sitting in his chair near the window, and managed to turn his head at the sound of her voice. She was certain he was smiling. "Sid, thank you for the lovely jewelry. I got it out of the safe-deposit box yesterday. I treasure every single piece." She held out the hand with the diamond ring. "And all that money. I don't need it." He frowned. "But I'll make good use of it." He made a fist once, an emphatic yes. She decided against telling him about the robbery. Besides, she'd never really liked pearls, even if they had come from him.

"Shall I read to you? Emmie says you like hearing her read." No.

"Let's talk about the old days, then. Remember that hardware convention in Chicago? The time that fellow had too much to drink at the banquet and fell down during his speech. What was his name? The big blond guy with the pretty wife who liked to party, too."

Sid made a sound, and Betty leaned close to him to try to understand. "Looo. Looo."

"Luisa! Right. And people used to call him Big Ed. Big Ed Gunderson. Wasn't he something? And the next year, in St. Louis, his exhibit collapsed, and I ended up helping him put it back together. Siddie was there that year."

For the next hour, Betty talked and Sid listened, nodding now and then as he remembered past events with her. "They had that big formal dance, and I wore a green dress you said you liked, and we danced all night. Don't think I could do that now."

Suddenly she tensed. She heard a door opening somewhere downstairs. Surely they weren't back from the funeral yet. Betty realized that she was frightened, convinced that whoever had killed Mary by mistake had come back to get rid of the right person. Poor helpless Sid. Not if she could help it.

"I'll be right back," she said. "Don't worry."

She went out to the hallway, desperately seeking some kind of weapon to defend herself. Nothing. But now she was certain she could hear voices below, and movement.

She opened one of the doors near Sid's room. It was clearly the room of Junior's teenage daughter, but somehow she didn't think that a larger-than-life-size poster of Eric Clapton constituted an adequate weapon for her defense. She tried the next door, the boy's room.

Here she found in-line skates, weights, and a pile of dirty underwear. She eyed the weights, which were sort of like small barbells, and lifted one. Heavy enough to do some damage, but she wasn't sure how accurate she'd be swinging it at a potential murderer's head.

Correction. If she heard voices, it meant more than one person was somewhere downstairs. Two people probably meant Bennie Mallis and Tom Crandell. She doubted whether she could handle those two. Perhaps the best she could hope for was the sudden return of the Edwards family and a large contingent of mourners. But there in the corner of the boy's room she saw something that gave her a little hope: a hockey stick. More easily wielded than the weights, if less heavy. She put the weights on the floor in the hall, since they might come in handy, and thought out a plan of attack. It would not be a good idea to be trapped in Sid's room, with two menacing men at the door, so she decided to stay here in the boy's room, ready to attack from behind.

Please don't let them hurt Sid, she thought, and hoped that Saint Jude was listening.

They must believe that Sid was at home alone. She'd made her arrangements with Mrs. Potter, who might not have mentioned her pending visit to Sid and Wendy, who had already left by the time she got here. If Sid was behind this, he couldn't have had a chance to pass on information about her presence. That gave her the weapon of surprise at least.

She listened intently behind the door, which was nearly but not quite closed, and after what seemed like a very long time, she heard them and held her breath. Heavy footsteps were coming up the stairs; there was a low rumble of voices, although she couldn't make out any words.

Her heart was pounding as she grasped the hockey stick. She heard them opening doors along the hallway, coming closer to Sid's door, and to her, and she was afraid. Then she wasn't. Nobody—nothing—was going to hurt her Sid, not while she was still breathing. If only the shock of their appearance in his room didn't bring on another stroke. Through the crack in the door she could see a person, but could not make out who it was. She squinted through her heavy glasses, but it did no good.

"Well, well, Mr. Edwards." It was Bennie's voice all right, and she opened the door a little wider to see Bennie standing in Sid's doorway, with Tommy at his back. Then they moved into the room, and Betty went into action.

She picked up one of the weights and ran down the hall to Sid, brandishing the hockey stick. She stopped abruptly at the open door and looked in. Sid was hunched down in his chair while Tommy and Bennie towered over him. She could read the terror in his face as he watched them.

"Can you hear me, old man?" Bennie was saying loudly. "It's me, Bennie Mallis—the guy you sent to prison over some lousy scrap metal that nobody wanted anyhow. My pal here and me are here to finish a job he screwed up on—killing the only person in this family who's ever been decent to me. Only he did the wrong one."

"Jeez, Bennie. It was an honest mistake. It was dark."

"Then you can make it right, Tommy. It's nice and bright in here now, and even a dummy like you can't make a mistake this time. I didn't make any mistake about the old Jap guy. Now hurry up. The people will be back any minute. Funerals don't last forever."

Betty edged into the room with the hockey stick aloft, praying that Sid would not see her and tell them about her presence by his expression. Sid, however, had his eyes glued to the two men and didn't even notice her. She saw the problem immediately. The hospital bed was between her and them, and to walk around it would surely attract their attention.

"Say your prayers, old man."

"He's sick, Bennie. He can't understand you."

"Mrs. Edwards said he could understand everything; he just can't talk." Bennie shook his head. "I shoulda been at her funeral today. Well, what are you waiting for?"

Tommy took a length of wire from his pocket and edged nearer to Sid.

It was too much for Betty. She let out a whoop. They turned quickly toward the door and started after her. On her way down the stairs, with Bennie and Tommy in pursuit, she dropped the weight, which bounced down a few steps and stopped. Tommy, who was coming down first, stepped on it and tumbled the rest of the way. Bennie, close behind him, couldn't stop himself and tripped over Tommy. The two landed in a heap at the foot of the stairs.

Betty raised the hockey stick and started to pound them as hard as she could. She was pleased to see that she'd drawn blood as Bennie's nose started to bleed. Tommy must have sprained his ankle, because he tried to stand and grab for her, but lost his balance and sank to the floor with a moan, clutching his ankle. With luck, she thought, he's broken his leg.

Betty was determined to keep up the beating until somebody came home. She found that her anger at their attempt to hurt Sid—indeed, murder him—was still boiling, but a part of her mind was very calm and business-like. It was an unpleasant job, but somebody had to do it. Elizabeth Ann Trenka never failed to do her duty.

Finally, blessedly, the front door opened and a horrified Wendy Edwards stood in the doorway. "Betty, what's going on?"

"Get Siddie in here! Get the police!" She was beginning to tire, and Bennie and Tom weren't yet entirely subdued. "They tried to kill Sid." Wendy withdrew quickly—to call the police, Betty hoped fervently.

"What the hell . . . ?" Junior burst in.

"Your hit men were trying again," Betty said. "They didn't succeed. Your father is okay."

"What are you talking about?"

Finally Betty lowered the hockey stick. "One of these two"—she poked Tommy with the hockey stick—"one of them murdered your mother by mistake. He was trying for Sid. They came back today while you were at the funeral to kill your father. Mrs. Potter asked me to sit with Sid this afternoon because she wanted to go to the funeral. But I wasn't going to let them get away with it . . . or you."

"Me?" Siddie had the good grace to look puzzled. "Why would I want to kill my own father?"

Betty shrugged. "The money, I suppose."

"The money is all under my control already," Junior said. "Mother was his guardian, and when she died, I inherited the job."

"So you didn't hire these two to do your dirty work?"

"Bennie works for me, sure. I don't even know who the other one is. And I wonder if you're not making up some silly story to show how devoted you are to my father."

"I think he'll confirm that they threatened him."

"Sorry, it won't wash. He can't talk."

"But his hearing is fine, and so is his understanding. He can answer yes and no by squeezing your hand with his left hand. Go upstairs and ask him anything you want, as long as he can answer the questions with yes or no. One squeeze for yes, two for no— At last!"

Wendy had called the police, and here they were.

Betty went upstairs to Sid while the others tried to explain, and the two men—who had not withstood Betty's determination very well—were hustled away.

Sid didn't look well.

"It's all right now," she said. "Wendy and Junior came home and they called the police." He gestured toward the orchid, which seemed to stand for Betty herself.

"Oh, I'm okay. You know I can handle almost anything." Sid actually nodded his agreement. "I think I might have damaged those two lads a bit with the skillful use of your grandson's hockey stick, but they'll survive. You'll survive."

He looked at her with a question in his eyes. "I don't know why, Sid. Or who. Siddie denies any intention to harm you, and I'm inclined to believe him. I have a bit of an idea—after putting some things together—but I'm not going to share it . . . not even with you. Siddie's going to be here soon to ask you what happened. Can you tell him if he asks the right questions?"

Sid reached out and took her hand, squeezing it once emphatically.

CHAPTER 21

IF SHE had been at home in East Moulton, she would have told Ted Kelso her theory and he would have listened intelligently. She wasn't sure that Cora and Dave were the right people to discuss the matter with. That left only Arnie Harris. At least he knew Bennie's history—and everything else about the Edwards family.

He wasn't at home, Sophie told her, but he was at Edwards & Son. Some kind of tax papers needed filing or such, and he'd heeded Linda's plea to come in since Mr. Edwards was attending the funeral.

"I need to talk to you, Arnie," Betty said when she reached him at the office. "Please don't leave until I get there. They—they tried to kill Sid." She heard her voice breaking.

"Just stay calm, drive carefully. I'll be waiting," Arnie said. "He's okay, though?"

"Thankfully yes. And I got the guys," she added modestly.

She arrived at Edwards & Son in good time, and went right to find Arnie, who as usual was engrossed in his ledgers.

"So begin," Arnie said. "I'm dying to know."

She explained about the aborted attack on Sid and her hockey stick exploits. "If they hadn't come home from the funeral, I'd probably still be there, whacking away. I've told the police what I think was going on, and now it's up to them to pin Mary's murder on Tommy, and Mr. Takahashi's murder on Bennie. Poor Miss Levenger. I do regret her taste in men."

"So what was behind it all?"

"They were hit men, as I speculated. Hired killers. At least Tommy was."

"And who hired him?"

"Technically, I guess it was Bennie Mallis—but the person who hired him was Mary Edwards."

Arnie appeared not to believe her. "But she was the one that got killed."

"This is what I suspect," Betty said. "I told you earlier how trapped she felt by Sid's condition, and how unhappy she was. He was standing in her way, so she arranged to have him killed. No big thing; he wasn't going to live forever anyhow. So she hires a hit man. How does she find such a person? There's a boy at her husband's company she's fond of, a rough type with criminal tendencies, shall we say? He was sent off to prison because of the husband, and when he's out, she asks him if he'll do this for her. She'll pay well."

"Betty, your imagination is running away—"

"No, listen. He won't do it himself. He'd be an obvious suspect given his relationship with Sid. But he knows someone who will—an old prison buddy. He'll work a deal with him, because the old prison buddy himself needs to get rid of someone who's standing in his way. And suddenly Mr. Takahashi is dead, strangled in his greenhouse, but not by the obvious person—his son-in-law Tommy Crandell—but by Bennie Mallis. Now it's Sid's turn to die, but the person coming to kill him—Tommy Crandell—makes a mistake. He doesn't know the Edwards house. He goes into the wrong room. Arnie, the hit man Mary Edwards hired to kill her husband murdered her instead."

"I don't know how you're going to prove that in court."

"Nevertheless, it's true. I overheard Bennie and Tommy talking about Tommy's 'mistake,' and how they were going to kill the right one this time. Mary spent a lot of time with Bennie, over at the luncheonette. There may be some way to trace her payment to him, if she paid him. And Miho Crandell saw the man who killed her father. Bennie is distinctive enough for her to remember him.

"If the proper psychological pressure is applied to those boys, I think one or another of them might crack. Bennie is pretty sentimental about Mary and doesn't like the idea of her being killed by accident by his pal."

Arnie sighed and leaned back in his chair. "As far as I'm concerned, nothing is beyond Bennie." He sat up. "What about your jewelry? Mary Edwards sure didn't have anything to do with that."

"That was probably Siddie's doing, don't you think? Sid tells Bennie to follow me to the bank, Bennie sees me come out of the bank with a large envelope, tells Sid, and Sid tells him to get it at any cost. He wants to know what I found in the safe-deposit box. It wasn't what he was hoping for, but I'll probably never see that stuff again. Never mind, I've got this." She waved the diamond ring. "And a couple of other things. I'm not big on accessorizing, even with real stones. You know what, Arnie? I think I'll empty a few more drawers of those filing cabinets. I want to finish up as early as I can tomorrow and see the visiting nurse about nursing homes for Sid. At least he's not in danger anymore. Then I'd like to go around to see him before I leave for East Moulton, tell him what I'm going to do about his care, things like that."

Betty got through the rest of the day, played cards— although not too well—with Cora and Dave, and explained her theory of Mary Edwards's death. Somehow, after having talked to Arnie about it, it was easy to tell them.

"It's like a TV movie," Cora said. "Who would have thought?"

"Maybe Mary saw a TV movie and got the idea," Betty said.

On Wednesday morning, she zipped through the last of the files, but *X*, *Y*, and *Z* held very little material in any case.

Sid stopped by the office where she was working and said, "We never thanked you properly for saving Dad's life. We won't forget it."

"It was nothing," Betty said. "And I was saving him more for me than for you."

"I understand. And thanks, too, for finding the business plan," Sid said. "I knew it was in those files somewhere, but I couldn't find it for the life of me. I don't know that I'll go ahead with the merger as Dad had laid it out, but it's given me something to think about. I'd hate to see Edwards and Son disappear. After all, I'm an Edwards, and I have a son, too."

"I can't help thinking what a blessing it is that he's athletic. Eric Clapton definitely wouldn't have done the job."

She glanced up to see him puzzling over that.

Betty said, "I'm looking into nursing homes for Sid today, and I'll let you know what I turn up so you can make a decision. I'll be stopping at your house later to say good-bye to Sid, then I'm off to East Moulton."

"I'll have Arnie send your fee when he makes out the checks next week. And Betty, thanks again."

After he left, she tossed the last sheets of paper into the wastepaper basket and went to the desk to put everything back in place. She stared for a long time at the manila envelope, carefully placed in the middle of the desk, read her name written in Sid's handwriting, saw that the envelope had been ripped open and resealed. Finally she picked it up and felt the shape of the boxes inside.

Sid Edwards Junior wasn't such a bad guy, after all. Rather more like his father than she would have believed. She hugged the envelope to her chest and said very softly, "Hi."

*If you enjoyed this Betty Trenka mystery,
don't miss the first two!*

THIS BUSINESS IS MURDER

by Joyce Christmas

Newly retired and already bored with her suburban
Connecticut neighborhood, Betty Trenka takes a
three-day temporary position at Zig-Zag, a small
computer firm.

Unexpectedly, she arrives in the midst of a murder
investigation—the highest ranking female
employee has just been killed. When a second
murder occurs, Betty combines her prodigious
office skills with the software savvy of a newfound
friend to solve the mystery—and discovers that
office politics can be deadly.

*Retired businesswoman Betty Trenka
figures that typing the memoirs
of a famous artist could be fun.*

DEATH AT FACE VALUE

by Joyce Christmas

That is, until she meets the ruthlessly vain artist
and his scantily clad girlfriend in their luxurious
rural Connecticut farmhouse.

But nothing prepares her for the violence about to
explode in her own backyard. Instead of a few
soothing weeks spent typing an artist's outrageous
memoirs, Betty is up to her keyboard in a deadly
investigation to track down a killer.

**Published by Fawcett Books.
Available at your local bookstore.**

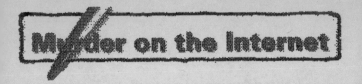